Dragon Blood 2: Wyvern

Dragon Blood 2
Wyvern

Avril Sabine

Cracked Acorn Productions
Australia

Dragon Blood 2: Wyvern

Published by

Cracked Acorn Productions

PO Box 1365

Gympie, Queensland 4570

Australia

978-1-925131-21-5 (Kindle)

978-1-925617-63-4 (EPUB)

978-1-925131-39-0 (Print)

Genre: Young Adult Urban Fantasy

It's still for you three.

Amber struggles to keep up with the constantly changing alliances amongst dragons and is worried Ronan, an ancient dragon, might not keep his end of the bargain they'd made. Life is filled with secrets and sometimes Amber just wants to get away from it all, which makes her jump at the chance to visit dragon lands. Her excitement over the visit is ruined when she learns someone wants her dead. And they're willing to pay her weight in gold to make their wish come true.

*

This story was written by an Australian author using Australian spelling.

Name Pronunciation

Like many names there is more than one way to pronounce the following ones. These are the pronunciations used in this series.

Names:

Alsandair (ahl-san-dare)

Anrai (arn-ree)

Bredon (bread-en)

Chait (single syllable, rhymes with hate)

Daray (dah-ray)

Doneele (donny-lee)

Emlyn (em-lin)

Gair (rhymes with hair)

Gethin (geh-thin)

Isleen (ish-lean)

Kiani (key-ah-knee)

Laren (lah-rin)

Maira (may-rah)

Orin (oh-rin)

Paili (pah-lee)

Queran (qwhere-rin)

Rhobert (row-bert)

Rian (ree-in)

Ronan (row-nen)

Tahmid (tar-mid)

Turi (two-ree)

Other pronunciations:

Erilan (era-len)

Feralenzi (fair-a-len-zee)

Pliethin (plea-thin)

Temolae (tem-oh-lay)

Chapter One

Amber kicked her bedroom door shut behind her. Grandmothers should be outlawed. Okay, maybe not all grandmothers. Her best friend Crystal had a grandmother who was perfect. It didn't seem fair she was stuck with one that could give little kids nightmares. Even getting her arm out of a cast nearly two weeks ago hadn't improved her grandmother's attitude.

Amber frowned as she stared at the curtains that didn't quite meet. She strode across the polished wooden floor and checked the French doors that were hidden behind them. They were closed, not locked. Had she locked them? She wasn't certain. No, the only thing she was certain about was that her grandmother's greatest joy in life was making everyone as miserable as her.

Staring through the glass, she checked the balcony.

Even in the dark she could see that no one was there. Nor could she sense or smell anyone. Letting go of the curtains, she glanced around her room. Everything seemed to be in its place. Her built-in wardrobe doors were shut, her schoolbag sat by the door, with several books scattered around it. Her laptop was closed and sitting on the desk in the corner and her duchess had the usual clutter of hairbrush, clips, scarves and hair ties overflowing the crystal tray in the middle.

"I'm getting paranoid," Amber muttered under her breath as she roughly slid open the door of her built-in wardrobe and grabbed a change of clothes. Shorts and a well-worn grey t-shirt. She'd given up wearing sleepwear this month. Her life was too unpredictable for that. Striding across the room to her ensuite, she slammed that door behind her too, hoping her grandmother heard the sound.

She dumped her clothes on the vanity. It was amazing she wasn't in therapy after putting up with her grandmother for nearly two months. How was she going to survive until the end of the year? That old woman was enough to drive anyone completely mad. Although, she probably wouldn't know when she did go crazy. Didn't even psychotic killers think they were sane?

Amber grabbed the hem of her t-shirt, about to pull it over her head so she could shower.

"Paranoia will help you stay alive."

Letting go of her t-shirt, Amber spun around, almost certain she'd sensed Ronan behind her for a moment. The bathroom was empty. Her brown eyes narrowed. "No games, Ronan."

A man seemed to step out of thin air. He was a lot taller than her and wore leather pants and a leather vest that showed off his muscular arms and broad chest. He looked to be in his thirties, but Amber knew he was a lot older. It showed in his eyes. Pale blue eyes that mirrored centuries of experience.

Amber put one hand on her hip, tilted her head and flicked her long chestnut hair, which fell in waves around her shoulders, out of the way. "I was just thinking about psychotic killers."

Ronan laughed. "You're always so entertaining."

"Yeah, yeah. So you keep saying. Now what are you doing in my bathroom? I'm sure it's not for the entertainment value."

"You need to disappear. Immediately."

Her arm dropped to her side and suspicion crossed her face. "Why?"

"Because maybe one of your gifts is prophecy."

Amber shook her head slightly. "You can't help

playing games, can you?" She really wasn't in the mood to deal with Ronan after an argument with her grandmother.

Ronan spread his hands and tried for an innocent look. His eyes spoiled it. "It's not like we know everything about Dragon Mages."

Amber took a deep breath and let it out slowly. Ronan was enough to turn anyone into a psychotic killer. Between him and her grandmother her sanity was probably on an endangered list. "Why are you here, Ronan? And I don't just mean in my bathroom. And cut the prophecy crap." She made each word separate and clear.

"Because there's a rumour that a contract has been put out on you."

She frowned. "Contract?"

Ronan nodded. "I believe that is what you humans call them."

Amber took a step back and shook her head. "This is even harder to believe than dragons being real. What next? Do you have your own version of the mob?"

"Your weight in gold is very tempting for many warriors. What do you weigh? Fifty kilos? Fifty-five?"

She could only shake her head. She didn't have a

clue exactly how much she weighed and right this minute she didn't think she wanted to find out. But not only that, she also didn't want to let Ronan see his words had unnerved her. Showing him weakness would be a very bad move. "Only about half a kilo when I'm a hawk. I can't see how tempting half a kilo of gold would be."

Ronan grinned. "When you die, you'll be human. Not a hawk or a panther."

Amber shrugged. "How do I know this isn't some trick or game of yours? And if it's not, how did you hear about the contract?"

"It's not a trick and I heard because I'm friends with some of my enemies."

Amber frowned. "That doesn't make sense."

"Of course it does. Now pack a bag and let's get out of here."

It had to be a trick. Ronan had to be planning something. "Why would someone want me dead?"

"Not just you. All Dragon Mages. But you're first on the list."

Amber could have sworn her heart stopped for several seconds before it began racing out of control. She stumbled backwards until she could sit on the closed lid of the toilet. Her legs suddenly felt like they were made of spaghetti. And it was well-cooked spaghetti with no chance of holding her up. "All?" She didn't even recognise her voice. Disbelief, fear and uncertainty were not her usual tone. "Crystal too? And Jay?"

"That's your biggest problem. I could turn you into the perfect warrior if it wasn't for your weakness where friends and family are concerned." Ronan leaned back against the wall, his arms crossing his chest.

Amber glared at him. "If you're an example of the perfect warrior you can forget it. I wouldn't eat the heart of my own son, if I ever had one."

"I'd suggest learning to be a little more ruthless. The ones who'll try to kill you won't be playing nice."

"We managed to beat you, didn't we?" Amber couldn't resist smiling, even though her heart still raced and the words 'not Crystal, not Jay' repeated over and over in her mind.

Ronan laughed. "Only because I wasn't trying to kill you. I needed you alive. I still do."

Amber's smile died instantly. "So what am I supposed to do?"

"Run. Hide."

"I can't. I've still got another few days of school left before the holidays."

Ronan pushed away from the wall. He dropped down in front of Amber so their eyes were level. "We're talking about your life. Do you understand that?"

"Yeah." Her voice was soft. "But what happens afterwards? My parents don't know anything about this. They'd freak. I'm still partly grounded from the last time I ran away and in this world I'm a kid and have to live by their rules."

"Then maybe you'd be better off leaving this world of yours and live in mine."

Amber frowned, her eyes narrowed again. She pushed Ronan from her so she could stand up. The past two months had brought enough changes to her life. No one was taking her world from her as well. "Is this a trick? Are you trying to get me to join you so I can help you with all your fights?"

"Would I do that?"

"Yes. And stop trying to look innocent. You were probably hatching plots when you were a baby."

Ronan laughed. "I'm sure I was at least a toddler before I started."

Amber gave him a scathing look. Her next comment was halted when she heard a noise in her bedroom. Had they found her already? She pushed past Ronan and swung the bathroom door open.

"Mum!" A glance behind showed Ronan disappearing into the Void. She stepped into her bedroom.

Donna put a pile of folded clothes on the bed and kept looking behind Amber. "Who's in the bathroom?"

Amber stepped out of the doorway to give her mother a clear view. "No one. Not even my reflection now." Lucky it hadn't been Kade. He couldn't disappear into the Void like Ronan could.

"Don't be smart with me, Amber." Donna stood in the doorway and pushed the door hard against the wall. Her gaze was drawn to every corner.

Amber crossed her arms over her chest, shifting her weight to her right leg. "Actually, it was a psychotic killer. I was just discussing with him the best way to murder Grandma."

Donna spun to face Amber, a finger pointed at her. "That's enough. This is your grandmother's home. Show her a little respect."

"I'll show her as much respect as she shows me."

"Keep this up and you can forget about your plans for the holidays. You're lucky you're not grounded for life after the stunt you pulled last month."

Amber struggled to hold her tongue. She wanted to tell her mother there hadn't been a problem until she'd been dragged away from her home and friends to Hicksville. But she didn't. She'd been warned that if she called the town by that name one more time she'd spend the school holidays in her room. Not many more days to get through. She just had to remember not to answer back. But that was getting harder and harder. Especially with the way her grandmother kept needling her. She knew it was deliberate. Her grandmother wanted her to be grounded. Although you'd think she'd be glad to have a break from her for two entire weeks.

"Well, Amber? What do you have to say for yourself?"

"Nothing," she muttered. What could she say without ending up permanently grounded? She turned her gaze to the floor and stared at the grain of the polished timber. How long was her mother going to stand there?

Donna finally sighed heavily. "I really don't know what to do with you some days, Amber."

Yeah, you and me both. Amber's jaw tightened as she bit back the comment.

Another heavy sigh and Donna retreated from the room, closing the door softly behind her.

"Do you want me to take care of your grandmother for you?"

Amber spun to face Ronan who was now near the French doors. "No!"

Ronan grinned. "You only have to ask. I'd be happy to help out."

"Leave my family alone." Amber glared at him. The sound of footsteps outside her room halted further words as she turned to see her door swing open again. "Now what do you want?" She hoped Ronan had returned to the Void.

"Don't be up half the night. You do have school tomorrow," Donna said.

"Yes, Mum." Amber couldn't resist the tone of exaggerated patience.

With one last look around the room Donna left, closing the door behind her.

Amber strode across her room and locked the door. Whatever had happened to knocking? Her mother had stopped doing that this past week. Did she suspect something?

Ronan returned from the Void, still near the French doors. "It's impossible to talk here. Meet me at one tomorrow morning."

What if she had more important things to do? Like sleep? "Where?"

"Your school. Alone."

"There's an assassin out to get all Dragon Mages,

with me right at the top of the list. And you want me to go traipsing around in the middle of the night on my own. How sane is that? Are you sure it wasn't you that hired them?"

Ronan's lips curved into a predatory smile. "I'd at least wait until I was finished with you." He laughed at her expression. "Don't worry. I keep my word. You're safe from me. You and yours. Now don't forget. Alone."

Before Amber could protest his order, he disappeared into the Void again. She growled in frustration. She wished she could disappear into the Void too. The best she could do was turn into a panther. Or a hawk. Not very helpful if you wanted to hide. And now this. Just when she was beginning to get the hang of being a Dragon Mage.

"Damn dragons. They think I've got nothing better to do other than run around after them." She growled again, this time sounding like an angry panther. And how did he expect her to get away from Kade? She checked the alarm clock beside her bed. He was due in ten minutes. Striding back to the ensuite, she slammed the door even harder than before, swearing as she did. It didn't make her feel any better.

Chapter Two

Amber checked the time on her phone again. Seven past one. She tucked it into the waistband of her black dragon-leather pants and folded her arms, glad for the dragon-leather jacket Kade had given her when the weather grew too cold for the vest she'd been wearing. All the leather they wore might make them look like they were part of some gang, but at least it saved her wrecking clothes when she shape-shifted. The dragon-leather was the only material that could survive the change.

Amber smiled slightly as she recalled when Kade had given her the jacket. It was light brown. She couldn't believe he'd recalled her snarky comment that she wanted clothing the colour of his dragon hide.

A sound behind her brought her back to the cold night and she spun, expecting to see Ronan. There was no one there. She scented the crisp air. Nothing. A slow perusal of the area gave the same results. Searching with her mind, she found not a single soul, dragon or human. Where was Ronan? And why the hell was he leaving her out in the open with no protection? She pulled out her phone again to check the time. Eleven past one. Damn inconsiderate dragon. Just because he was centuries old didn't mean he could make everyone jump the moment he spoke.

She started to pace. If he didn't hurry she was out of here. She couldn't stay after two anyway. By then Kade and Maira would know she'd tricked them into leaving her alone. Unprotected. Another sound had her spinning in the opposite direction. Nothing.

When Ronan finally arrived, she was going to kill him. Slowly. Who was she kidding? She wouldn't be able to get close enough. But she could dream. "Damn it, Ronan. You've got five minutes and then I'm out of here." She spoke loudly, but didn't shout. Dragons had good hearing whether they were in dragon or human form. If he wasn't close enough to hear her threat then she wasn't sticking around on her own.

Another visual search of the area showed nothing. Where was he? Was he coming? She looked at the time again and then put her phone away. That was it. She'd given him more than enough time. Amber started to stride towards the school gate.

A rush of movement caused Amber to spin and block the man who leapt out of the shadows at her. A flurry of punches followed the initial attack and she ducked as many as she could, blocking the rest. Another shadow flew at the man, pushing him into the wall of the school building with a grunt and a thud. Heart in her throat, Amber drew in a steady breath as she recognised Ronan.

"What was that?" Ronan demanded, his hand holding the man pinned to the building by his throat. "Do you call that an attack? You put no effort into it."

"I have no excuse."

Hearing his words, Amber looked him over carefully. He had sandy blond hair pulled back from his face and when Ronan let him go, she saw it was tied at the nape of his neck. He was a similar size and build to Ronan. That put him at a little over six foot with far too many muscles for Amber to have beaten him if he'd really been trying to kill her.

"Who are you?" Amber's gaze travelled over the bare chest, which made her wonder how he tolerated the cold and then stared at the tattoo that covered the muscles of his upper left arm. It was a Celtic trinity knot with three dragons bursting out of the edges.

When the man didn't answer her, she met his gaze in query. Her mouth dropped open when she saw pale blue eyes the same as Ronan's. Without thinking, she threw her fist towards Ronan and fleetingly wondered how she managed to get pushed face first against the building Ronan had held the man against.

"Not a smart move. Did you really think I'd let you hit me?" Ronan let her go.

Amber turned to face him, supporting herself against the wall, her heart racing a million kilometres an hour. "Who is he? Another one of your sons?"

"Rian. The one that managed to get his arse kicked by your dragons. He was laid up for a month. He'll teach you to fight if he wants to make up for that mess."

Amber looked between the two men. "I don't need his help."

Ronan pulled a gun out and pressed it at Rian's forehead. "In that case, he's of no use to anyone."

"What!" Amber went from scared to angry in a second. "What do you think you're doing, Ronan? Are you trying to manipulate me?" She couldn't believe Rian stood there, his expression still neutral, his gaze meeting that of his father.

"I don't bluff."

"You can't do this." Amber's mouth dried and she

desperately tried to think of a way to stop this nightmare.

"Then you do want him?" Ronan turned his gaze on Amber.

She could only nod. Her gaze was still on Rian and she could have sworn she saw a moment of relief in his gaze.

"You'll fight him like you mean it. Or I'll shoot him." Ronan's expression was harsh. "Even to aiming for the wings if you're throwing fire at him. If he can't get out of the way he doesn't deserve to live."

"That's harsh." Amber couldn't believe Rian still stood there, expressionless. She'd have made several comments by now if it had been one of her parents talking about her like this. And none of them would have been complimentary.

"Only the strong survive. I wouldn't be doing him any favours if I didn't teach him that. Eventually you'll learn too." Ronan tucked his gun into the back of his leather pants.

"Not likely."

"Then you'll die, but not until I'm finished with you." Ronan gestured towards his son. "And he'll make sure you live long enough to help me or I'll tear his heart out with my own hands."

"Bastard," Amber muttered.

Ronan smiled as if he'd been complimented. "Don't forget it." He glanced around. "Let's get out of this depressing place."

"You were the one who wanted to come here."

"If you hadn't been so impatient it might have been worthwhile."

"Why'd you want to come here anyway?"

"It doesn't matter."

"Of course it does." Amber crossed her arms over her chest. "Why here?"

"To give the assassins a chance to find you."

It took a couple of seconds for Ronan's words to sink in. "What!"

"Oh stop with all the drama." Ronan turned from her and began to move away from the building.

Amber grabbed him by the arm and wasn't surprised when Ronan shook her off with a look of annoyance. "Talk to me. I'm not one of your sons who'll stand around while you get them killed."

"If they followed orders better they wouldn't get killed."

"Ronan!"

"We only have rumours. I need to find out who and why. And you can't retaliate until an attempt has been made."

"Attempt?" Amber hated how Ronan had the

ability to make her voice sound like that of a scared little girl.

Ronan laughed. "Don't you like that? Too bad. You're a part of our world, you have to live by its laws." He looked over at Rian. "Guard her and train her." He leapt into the air and, turning into a blue and silver dragon, disappeared into the night.

Amber growled in frustration. She had more questions. How dare he take off like that? She heard movement behind her and turned to face Rian. What was she going to do with him? And why did he just stand there watching her? "What?"

"I have no idea what you are asking."

"Why are you standing there?"

"Guarding you."

Amber started to tell him he could leave, then recalled she was alone, at school, after midnight and there were assassins after her. She nodded her head. When she got home she'd tell him to leave. Without talking, she turned into a hawk and flew towards the balcony of her second storey room. If she hurried, she could make it back home before Kade knew she was gone.

She could see her balcony only metres away when a bellow echoed in her mind. *"Amber! Where are you?"*

She sighed as she landed on her balcony and turned

human. Rian dropped down beside her, changing in mid air from a large blue dragon, with bronze and silver flecked wings, to a human. The balcony door swung open before she could answer.

Kade filled the doorway, his hands holding the doors open, his expression fierce. "Where were you? And who's that?"

Amber met Kade's golden brown eyes, the same colour as the sun-streaked strands of his brown hair. "He's one of Ronan's sons."

Kade's eyes narrowed. "Didn't you attack us last month?"

Rian nodded.

"Then what are you doing here? What's Ronan up to?"

Amber pressed her hand against Kade's chest, pushing her way into the room. "It's too cold to stand out on the balcony all night." She heard Rian follow her in and close the door. Her gaze never left Kade's. What should she tell him? And how should she? He was going to be livid.

"Just get it over with. If Ronan's involved I doubt I'm going to like a single word you have to say. And why is he still hanging around?" Kade gestured towards Rian who took up a post in the corner closest to the French doors.

Amber strode towards her bed, discarding her jacket along the way to reveal a black, dragon-leather vest. "Apparently I need an extra bodyguard." She decided to avoid mentioning Rian was also meant to train her to fight. And from what Ronan had said, Rian was to be the practice dummy.

"Why do you need an extra guard?" Kade's voice held more than a hint of impatience.

"What would my weight in gold be worth in real dollars?"

Kade frowned. "What?"

"Between two and three million depending on your exact weight and the current dollar value of gold."

Amber dropped onto her bed at Rian's words. "Two million?" She closed her eyes a moment then met Rian's pale blue eyes that were unnervingly like his father's. "Dollars?"

Rian nodded. "If you give me your weight I can find an exact figure for you. But the market value does fluctuate."

Amber shook her head, words beyond her. She lay back on her bed and stared at the pattern her bedside lamp made on the ceiling.

Kade sat beside her. "What have you done now?" The impatience was replaced by weariness.

"I didn't do anything. Apparently someone thinks my death is worth my weight in gold."

"Since when?" Kade grabbed her by the shoulders, pulling her up to face him. "What were you doing running around town at this hour if you have assassins after you? Are you insane?"

"Obviously. I talk with dragons, think I can turn into a panther or hawk at will and throw balls of fire from my hands. No one sane does that." She avoided mentioning her ability to heal since Rian was standing in the corner and Ronan still didn't know she could do that.

"Tell me everything. From the start. And you better not leave anything out."

Amber sighed and recounted her day, warily watching as Kade tried to control his anger when she mentioned meeting Ronan after she'd been told of the assassins. "What I can't understand is why anyone would be willing to pay two million dollars for my death. Or even why I'd be first on their list."

"The only difference I can see between you, Jay and Crystal is you spend time with Ronan." Kade turned towards Rian. "What do you know about it?"

"More now than I did earlier."

"Your father's such a bastard," Amber said to Rian.

Rian nodded, not seeming to be the least offended.

"Then why do you help him?" Amber frowned. "I'd be miles in the opposite direction from him if I was you."

"He'd rip my heart out."

Amber was made speechless again. She couldn't understand how Rian could be so calm about the prospect. Or even how Ronan could be so hard on his sons. She shook her head, unable to think of anything to say.

Rian smiled fleetingly, his serious expression lightening considerably. "It is the way it has always been for me. Ronan will accept nothing other than unquestioning loyalty. He expects no more from us than he expects from himself. And as his youngest son, I am of least value."

"Oh, your mother was that dragon with the Gold in her lineage he captured a couple of decades ago. People still talk about that," Maira said as her and Brann came through the French doors. "Apparently Ronan was so mad he nearly killed you and your mother when you were born with no Gold in you. How many other kids did he end up having with her?"

"Six girls. No Golds."

"What's wrong with you people?" Amber leapt to her feet. "He kidnapped a woman and had her long enough for her to have seven kids to him. Why didn't anyone rescue her?"

Only Rian bothered to answer. "She escaped once she was pregnant with me, but chose to go back when I was born with bronze in my wings. They both thought it might mean they were getting close to Gold."

"But why? I mean, he'd kidnapped her."

"Because it's the Gold Dragons who rule." Maira strode across the room and knelt at Kade's feet then sat back on her legs. "I'm sorry I left Amber unprotected." Chunky silver and black bracelets glinted as she pressed her arms against the floor. Green eyes were lowered and her head was bowed till it touched the polished timber of the floor. Her black hair, which was cut level with her mouth, swung forward and her skin seemed even darker against the golden timber of the floor.

"Oh, get up. It was my fault, Maira." Amber tried to tug her up. Brann stepped forward to prevent her. He was around six foot, with curly brown hair touching his shoulders, deep blue eyes and for a change his friendly grin was replaced with a serious expression. "Let me go, Brann." Amber tried to pull away from him. Seeing Rian move for the first time, she sent a glare towards him. "And you stay out of this."

"Leave her," Kade said to Brann who immediately let Amber go. "I'll deal with this later, Maira. Get up."

"There's nothing to deal with." Amber's hands went to her hips and her expression dared Kade to argue.

Kade ignored her and turned to Maira.

Amber guessed they were communicating in their minds and she worried her actions had caused problems for Maira. Kade was her last chance to serve a Gold Dragon. "If you get rid of Maira I'll never talk to you again."

"Right this moment I'm beginning to think that'd be a good thing," Kade glared back at Amber.

"Footsteps."

All gazes turned towards Rian before they stared at the door leading into the hallway. Amber silently rushed to the door to check it was locked. A sigh of relief escaped when she found it was. The door handle rattled and Amber held her breath.

"Are you awake in there, Amber? Why's your light on?"

Maira lightly ran into the bathroom and flushed the toilet, grinning at Amber who nodded in understanding.

She moved away from the door before she spoke. "Can't I even go to the toilet in peace?"

There was a moment of silence. "How long do you need to leave your light on?"

"I was waiting until you finished talking to me." Amber glanced towards Kade who was closest to her lamp. He reached out and turned it off. "Happy?"

"Goodnight, Amber."

"Night, Mum." Amber stood in the darkness, listening to her mother return to her own room. Her eyes quickly adjusted to the lack of light and she was glad of the panther's ability to see at night. "You all have to go. I can't afford to be grounded."

"No one's going anywhere. Do you have any idea what that amount of money will do?" Kade demanded.

"Hire an assassin. Obviously." Amber made sure her tone made it clear she didn't appreciate him talking to her like she was an idiot.

"Do you know how many landless Gold Dragons there are? Two million dollars will gather a large enough army with which to capture lands. And once a Gold Dragon is old enough and has captured a Pliethin, they can eventually walk through the Void," Kade said softly. "You won't notice them until they're right there next to you, about to attack."

Amber could have sworn she heard the ocean roaring in her ears and she knew her heart must have stopped for at least half a minute. Her breathing certainly did because suddenly she was light headed and had to take a deep breath. She remembered how it had felt when Ronan had come out of the Void with a knife at her throat and his arm wrapping around her chest so it had been impossible to escape.

"Do you understand now, Amber?" Kade crossed the few paces that were between them.

Amber tilted her head up, straightening her shoulders. No one, absolutely no one, was going to make her go running scared. Not Ronan, not Kade's warrior brother Flinn and certainly not some faceless assassin. "Let them try."

The silence was broken by Rian's sharp laugh. "No wonder Ronan adores you."

"Yeah, well, I can live without his adoration." Amber felt tired all of a sudden. She glanced at her alarm clock. It was after three and she had to get up at seven. "I'm going to bed. I don't care what the rest of you do." She grabbed the clothes she'd tossed on the bed earlier and retreated to the bathroom to change out of her leather. She forced herself to quietly close the door when she'd have much preferred to slam it.

Chapter Three

A banging on her bedroom door woke Amber much sooner than she would have preferred. "Yeah. I'm awake." She didn't open her eyes. It was the last thing she wanted to do. Beside her on the bed, she felt Kade change from dragon back to human. A pity he couldn't stay in human form while he slept since as a dragon he didn't leave much space in the queen-sized bed for her. But since dragon was their base form, in sleep and in death, that was what they turned into.

"Then sound like you're awake or I'll come in there and drag you out of bed. This is the third time you've told me you're awake this morning."

Amber quickly sat up at her mother's words. Third? Surely she was kidding. This was the first call she remembered hearing. Her eyes squinted as she tried to make out the numbers on her alarm clock. Nearly eight. Amber jumped out of bed and almost stepped on Rian who hurriedly rolled out of her way. She frowned at him. What was he doing sleeping on her floor? But then again, she guessed he wasn't sleeping since he was still human.

"Amber? You haven't gone back to sleep, have you?"

"I'm up. I'll be down as soon as I shower."

"If I don't hear the water start within the next five minutes I'll be back with a key to open this door," Donna warned.

Amber swore under her breath as she hurriedly grabbed her uniform as well as dragon-leather shorts and vest to wear underneath in case she needed to change into a panther or hawk. Just before she shut the door to her ensuite, Amber turned back to Kade who was sitting on the edge of her bed, stretching. "Where are Maira and Brann?"

"Getting the car to give you a lift to school."

Amber nodded and then shut the door on him. She leaned against the closed door, trying not to think of all she'd learned yesterday. Assassins. It didn't seem real. Certainly not with a two million dollar price on her head. And three million was completely unbelievable. She couldn't even imagine it. She bit back a sigh, knowing the two dragons in her bedroom would hear it, stripping off her clothes as she turned on the water. And to think she'd started to believe life wasn't quite so bad here. Now it just totally sucked.

* * *

After what had probably been the longest school day in the history of man, Amber found herself seated at the kitchen table at Kade's house that he shared with Maira and Brann. The room was crowded. Seated at the table with her was her brother Jasper, her best friend Crystal, Kade, Flinn, Maira and Brann. Flinn had protested Maira and Brann at the table when his warriors had left the kitchen to do guard duty, which was expected of them. Several steps behind Amber's chair, Rian stood guard over her, an acceptable place according to Flinn. They'd been discussing the situation for the past hour, if yelling could be considered discussion. But if the look on Flinn's face was anything to go by, it had been one hour too many.

He sprang to his feet and slammed his hands flat against the table, glaring at Kade across from him. Flinn had short brown hair and blue eyes. He wasn't as good looking as the other dragons at the table, but there was something about him that made you look twice. And then want to give him a wide berth. An air of danger that he communicated in the way he held himself and spoke. "She already is bait. All we'd be doing is taking advantage of the situation."

"You're not going to use her as bait," Crystal argued before Kade had a chance to continue his argument.

"Will. You. Shut. Up." Flinn glared at Crystal, making her flinch.

"Don't talk to her like that." Amber dropped her arm around Crystal, who sat beside her. "She doesn't have to continue to be your mage."

Flinn turned his glare on Amber. "If you really wanted to protect her you'd willingly be bait."

"You do realise we've been going around in circles with this conversation." Jasper was the only one who seemed calm.

"It's not like she can see the future and tell us who's after her," Flinn snarled. "We don't have any other choice."

"Prophecy!" Amber turned to look at Rian. "That's what Ronan wanted. He wants me to lie and say I can see the future."

Rian shook his head. "He does not believe you could pull it off. You are too honest."

"Sometimes," Maira muttered.

"I said I was sorry about tricking you," Amber said.

Flinn hit the tabletop again. "Can we focus? You can go on Oprah and talk about how sorry you are for all I care, as long as it's not when I'm around. Now what about the wyvern nest? Are we still leaving Friday so we can clean it out these holidays?"

Crystal rose to her feet, glaring at Flinn. "You're unbelievable. Amber's life is under threat and all you can think about is passing your stupid warrior tests."

"Can we protect Amber better on clan lands?" Jasper asked.

"I think so." Kade turned towards Crystal. "Sit down."

Crystal gestured towards Flinn. "When he does."

"This is worse than dealing with prep students." Jasper's words drew a glare from both Crystal and Flinn. He shrugged. "Hey, I'm only telling it like it is."

Crystal sat when Flinn did. "I still think we should tell Kade's mum. We need more guards."

"Just what we need. More landless Gold Dragons in the perfect position to collect the bounty," Flinn said.

"Kiani wouldn't send someone untrustworthy," Crystal protested.

"Trust no one. How many times have I got to tell you that?" Flinn asked.

"A small group of guards that have nothing to gain from the situation is best," Rian said.

Amber had finally had enough. She didn't know how many times the conversation would circle around with nothing being solved, but she was over it. Rising to her feet, she started to move away from the table, Rian at her heels.

"Where are you going?" Kade asked.

"Anywhere but here. We're getting nowhere." Amber strode from the room, ignoring the chaos she left in her wake. Let them continue their arguments without her. She passed through the hall, into the lounge and paused at the front door. Morgan, one of Flinn's warriors, leaned against a verandah post. He ignored Amber as she went to the far end of the verandah. She didn't want any company.

For weeks she'd been looking forward to visiting dragon lands. Now someone had ruined her school holidays. Instead of enjoying two weeks away from her grandmother, she would be stuck looking over her shoulder, waiting for someone to stab her in the back. Or maybe they'd shoot her. Ronan certainly had a fondness for guns. There were probably other dragons that did. Or how about a sniper? Amber scanned the area nervously.

The old house was surrounded by open paddocks that were dotted with gum trees. It was typical Queensland farming country and far from the city Amber had grown up in, and loved. She sighed, wishing she could go home. And not to her grandmother's house where her mother had dragged her to, for what was supposed to have been only six weeks. She wanted to be in the city, with her father, back in the house she'd been raised in. She wanted to go back to Brisbane with Jasper and Crystal when they returned. Instead, she was stuck here until the end of the year when she finished year twelve. And they weren't even halfway through the school year yet. Not for another five days anyway.

Kade stepped up beside her and leaned on the verandah rails. Amber waited for him to speak. When he remained silent, she looked over at him.

"I'm sorry I've messed up your life so much."

Amber shook her head. *"It was an accident."*

"Not quite." Kade smiled.

"What do you mean?"

"If I'd been paying attention I wouldn't have been

caught off guard by the wyvern. And I wouldn't have ended up bleeding all over your bedroom floor."

"Are you finally going to tell me what distracted you?"

"I was watching this gorgeous girl standing on her balcony staring up at the stars."

"Great. So it was all my fault."

Kade laughed. *"No, it wasn't."* He stepped forward, drawing her into his arms. *"It's no one's."* His lips brushed across hers, but she pulled away.

"We've got an audience."

"I bet I could make you forget them."

Amber shook her head, pulling away further. "What was decided?"

"Other than you'll still be collected from your home Friday afternoon by a limo?"

"Yeah."

"Nothing."

"And what else?"

"We guard you."

Amber leaned against the verandah rails. "I'm not sitting around waiting for someone to attack me."

Rian stepped forward. "Ronan said that when you fail to come up with a plan to tell you to ring him. He has one."

"Like the last one? Lure her somewhere deserted and alone and let her be attacked?" Kade demanded.

"She was never alone. There were four Gold Warriors, two of my brothers, Ronan and myself."

"Well it certainly wasn't working." Amber wondered where Rian and his brothers had been. As far as she knew they couldn't walk the Void since they weren't Gold and she hadn't sensed them when she'd searched.

Rian shrugged. "You did not give it a chance."

"We aren't interested in anything Ronan has to say." Kade folded his arms across his chest.

Rian held a business card out to him. "Ronan will be at this address, in the city, Friday night. After that…" he shrugged. "He might not be so keen to help."

Seeing Kade wasn't going to take the card, Amber did. She noticed the address was in one of the wealthier suburbs. Wealth. She frowned. Would it be possible to figure out who could afford to pay out more than six million dollars in gold to get rid of the three of them?

"What are you thinking?" Kade asked.

"Who could easily afford to pay that size bounty?"

Kade shrugged. "Quite a few people."

"Twenty-three."

Amber stared at Rian. "How do you know?"

"Ronan has already tried to figure it out that way.

And that does not include the clans or even the individuals who would work together to come up with the bounties."

Amber turned to look out over the paddocks again. "Is this what life's always going to be like?"

"Only until we can prove it isn't worth the trouble going against us," Kade said.

Amber was sure she wasn't going to like the answer, but she had to ask the question. "How do we do that?"

"Survival of the fittest."

Yep, she'd been right. "I'm beginning to hate that phrase," she muttered. She could almost understand why Ronan had at times killed those who annoyed him. Causing serious bodily harm to the next person who spoke those words was becoming very tempting.

Chapter Four

Amber felt like she was a nervous wreck. Every sound, every movement in the past two days had nearly driven her insane. She kept expecting assassins to leap out of every shadow and was sick and tired of never having a moment alone. She'd drawn the line at someone guarding her in the bathroom. If an assassin killed her in there at least it'd save her from having to die of embarrassment.

"Are you ready?"

Amber jumped at Maira's words. She forced herself to calmness. "Ready to be committed more like."

Maira laughed. "You'll be all right. We'll get you to clan lands and hole up in one of the castles Kade's family own."

"I'm sick of telling all of you I won't be locked away while you deal with the wyverns."

"Don't worry about it. Everything's under control," Maira said soothingly.

Amber gritted her teeth. If she heard that phrase one more time she was likely to flatten the next person who said it. And with the lessons Rian was giving her she should make a good job of it. She looked over to the corner to check if Rian was still there. He was as silent and still as ever. It was easy to forget he was there sometimes.

A sharp knock at the front door had Amber grabbing her bags and rushing downstairs. She knew Rian would exit her room through the French doors and she could hear Maira run down the stairs behind her. Amber bit back a sigh. Never alone.

Donna stood at the foot of the stairs. "Make sure you ring me every day."

"Mum!"

"You're still only sixteen, Amber."

Amber grinned fleetingly. "I won't be when I come home."

Donna frowned. "I'm still not sure you should be away for your birthday."

"Jay will be there with me. I'm sure he can manage to say happy birthday."

"We're going to have a party for her. And Brann as

well. His birthday is two days later, on the twelfth of July," Maira said.

Amber quickly gave her mother a hug, worried she might change her mind. "See ya, Mum. One of us will ring each day." Kade had got their mobile phones altered so they'd work in his world. She rushed towards the door and nearly collided with her grandmother.

"There's a limousine at the front door." Helen appeared extremely delighted. "I wonder how many of the neighbours noticed."

At a look from her mother, Amber quickly gave her grandmother a hug. "See you." She rushed outside, Maira on her heels as she reached the limousine. The door was held open for her by a uniformed chauffeur and she smiled when she saw Rian already seated. Her bags were taken from her and she turned to wave to her family as she climbed into the vehicle. Donna called out last minute instructions, her words muffled by the closing door.

Amber looked out the back window, as they drove off, and watched as Donna continued to wave until they turned a corner. She faced forward so she could get comfortable. "I can't believe I made it to Friday."

Maira laughed. "Yeah, I thought a few times there you'd make a comment that would get you grounded. But don't worry. Kade has a small castle where you can hide for the next two weeks."

"And then what?"

"What do you mean?"

"What happens if we don't find out who's trying to have me killed?"

"Oh, I see what you mean. That's no problem. Kade has the use of the castle as long as he needs it."

Maira's words caused a feeling of dread to wash over her. Was Kade going to keep her locked up forever? Surely not. Maira must be mistaken. "How long does Kade plan for us to stay there?"

"Until the people who put a contract on your life are found."

"And how does he plan to find them?"

Maira shrugged. "I never asked. But I'm sure he'll figure something out."

"Well, he better be quick because these school holidays are only two weeks long."

"Jay said there's always distance education. So you don't have to worry about finishing year twelve."

Amber stared at Maira. "Jay's been helping plan this?" She was going to kill her brother. Right after she finished dealing with Kade.

Maira nodded.

Anger burned through Amber. They were not

going to take her from her world. Even if they thought it was the best thing for her. Without looking at him, she sent her thoughts to Rian. *"What's Ronan's plan?"*

"Drawing the assassins out so we can catch them. He believes he can make them talk."

Amber fell silent. Two choices. Be locked away in a castle for who knew how long or, follow Ronan's plan that if past experience was anything to go by, probably consisted of her being bait. Hide or face her enemy. She'd never been any good at hiding. The other alternative didn't sound appealing either. Although if anyone could pull off a stunt like that, it'd probably be Ronan. She glanced at Maira. There was no way she'd be able to convince Maira that going to Ronan's was a good idea. It looked like it'd have to be trickery again. She only hoped it didn't cause more problems between Maira and Kade.

Amber leaned her head back, closing her eyes. For now she could only wait. Time dragged slowly. Night eventually fell, and they were on the outskirts of the city when an opportunity came. The chauffeur stopped for petrol and when he left to pay for it, Amber turned to Rian. "Can you grab me an ice cream?" She met his gaze. *"Refuse me."*

"I am your bodyguard. I cannot leave you alone. Send Maira."

She turned to Maira. "Can you please? I'd go myself, but with the way everyone carries on lately…" Amber let her words trail off.

"We'll send the chauffeur as soon as he's back from paying for the fuel," Maira said.

"I want to pick Jay and Crystal up so I can get out of this vehicle. I want to stretch my legs and I know neither of you will let me do that." Amber kept her gaze on Maira, speaking directly to Rian. *"A little help here."*

"It is not safe for you to go wandering about," Rian said.

"Oh, all right. I won't be long," Maira grumbled as she got out of the limousine and shut the door.

"What are you planning?" Rian asked.

"I need to see Ronan." Amber pulled her long sleeved dress over her head, her dragon-leather pants and vest were on underneath it. She grabbed out a pen and piece of paper and wrote 'sorry' on it. *"Follow if you can."* She changed into a hawk. *"And open the door for me. It's a little beyond what I can manage in this body."* As soon as the door was open, Amber checked that Maira and the chauffeur weren't looking in her direction before she flew out of the vehicle and into the sky.

From above, she saw Rian dash across the road and between two buildings. He streaked into the sky, a blur of movement humans would have missed. When she saw he followed after her, she headed for the address on Ronan's business card. Moments later, Maira frantically broadcast Amber's name. She ignored her. She didn't want to give her a direction to head in. They'd figure it out soon enough. That was if Kade recalled the address on the card he'd refused to take. If Amber could have grinned she would have.

That'd teach them to try and cage her. She swooped at a pigeon she flew past and watched as it dodged away. A quick movement and she had it in her talons. It had been too easy. She let it go, overriding the hawk's instinct to make a meal of it. She was no one's pigeon to be easily caught. If they wanted to come after her she'd show them what they could do with their survival of the fittest rule. It was going to be survival of the smartest and they'd soon see she wasn't lacking in that area.

Unaccustomed to flying long distances, Amber was relieved to see Ronan's house. Rian led her to a rooftop garden where she could change into her human form. Ronan was lazing on a couch amongst the plants when they arrived. She glanced at Rian, but as usual, his expression was unreadable.

"Where's the entourage?" Ronan glanced around. "I was beginning to think you couldn't go anywhere without them."

Amber ignored Ronan's comment and sat in an empty chair across from him. "Explain your plan."

"Lovely weather we've been having and I know it's terribly rude to drop in unannounced, but I had missed seeing you so much."

Amber wasn't in the mood. The past few days had worn out any good humour she possessed. "Oh shut up, Ronan. You invited me. Now do you have a plan or am I going to leave again?"

"Manners never hurt. It seems like you have them for everyone but me."

Amber glanced towards Rian and wondered what tales he'd been telling Ronan. And he was right. She wasn't usually this rude, but she had a very good excuse. She was sick of looking over her shoulder waiting for someone to attack her.

"I'm tired. It's been a long week and when have you ever bothered to ask me how I'm doing? Cut the crap and get to the point." Amber stared at Ronan, waiting to see how he'd take her comment. It was probably crazy to bait him, but if it was one thing she'd learned, Ronan hated weakness and pounced on it like a cat on a mouse. She wanted to be a mouse as much as she wanted to be a pigeon.

"I'll send out several messages to places you could possibly be, letting them think I don't know where to find you. That way we'll have a greater chance of at least one message being intercepted. I believe there's someone already planted in the castle Kade plans to take you to. In the message I'll give the time and location of where we'll meet and allow you to bring one bodyguard." Ronan gestured towards Rian. "I daresay they'll try and take him out first, but if he lets anything happen to you he better hope they kill him." He sent a warning look to his son before he returned his gaze to Amber. "You, I will get to safety, while my Gold Warriors come out of the Void and catch the assassin."

"It sounds simple enough, but how do you know it'll work?" Amber asked.

"Because I've done my homework."

"Then what happens after that? You'll only have the assassin, not the person who ordered the contract."

Ronan smiled, a highly predatory smile. "Then you can go off on your wyvern hunt while I see what the assassin knows. Two of my Golds will take turns to shadow you while you're there."

She couldn't help thinking that Ronan's smile didn't bode well for the assassin. "And if the assassin knows nothing?"

"Then we keep going until we find one that does."

"And what about when the school holidays are over? What then?"

"What about them?" Ronan looked towards Rian for clarification. He smiled at what Rian must have told him in his mind. "Then Rian will return you to your grandmother's home. That is what you wanted?"

Amber nodded.

"My Golds will return with you. But tell me something." Ronan rose to his feet and stopped in front of her to place a hand on each arm of her chair. "Why haven't you involved Kiani?"

Amber forced herself not to draw back from him. "What's your price for your help?"

"I need you to stay alive until my castle is captured."

Amber smiled, trying to remain calm even though her senses screamed at her to run from Ronan and his piercing gaze. "I can afford to pay that."

"What did Kiani want?"

"Why would I pay any price that's higher than the one you ask?"

Ronan moved even closer. "You have years to go before you have the experience to try and bluff me. What's her price for helping?"

Amber winced as Kade broadcast her name. Ronan pushed away from her and strode to the open area of his rooftop garden. Six dragons and two hawks flew down to land in front of him, all quickly becoming human. Amber forced herself to remain in her seat, trying to appear relaxed. They couldn't make her go to the castle, and they couldn't keep her there. She glanced at Rian who moved to stand just behind her. For some reason, that action helped her to actually relax a little. She waited in her seat, watching as Kade strode towards her.

"What did you think you were doing?"

"I'm not some pigeon to be locked away in a cage." Amber rose to her feet, sick of everyone towering over her.

"Then what? You throw your life away? That isn't acceptable."

"I wasn't trying to." Amber saw Flinn prevent Crystal from joining them, a whispered argument followed that her brother joined.

"Don't you understand? With the current price of gold, the bounty is worth nearly three million dollars."

Amber ignored the thread of fear that curled through her. "Then I guess they better hurry up and get the job done in case the market falls."

"I'm trying to keep you safe."

"I'm not your responsibility."

"Jay said-"

"I'm not his either. You can't plan my life for me." Amber glared at Kade.

He finally nodded. "I'll include you in the plans."

"No. You'll make suggestions and I'll decide on the plan."

"That isn't-"

"My life. Remember?"

Kade sighed, then nodded. "We'll give it a try. But I'm not going to stand back and let you do something stupid."

Amber grinned wryly. "If you ask my parents, that's all I ever do."

Kade's lips slowly curved into an answering smile. "Does this mean we can kiss and make up now?"

Amber glanced at the group of people who quietly watched them and probably listened. "I'll think about it." She started to move past Kade but he reached out to stop her, still smiling.

His lips were close to her ear, his words quieter than a whisper. "I had plans for tonight. Did you want me to suggest them to you now so you can decide if you like them."

Amber ignored the heat his words generated. "I have a plan to run by you." She looked towards Ronan and then back at Kade.

"And I guess I'm not going to like this plan."

Amber grinned. "Probably not since it doesn't involve me being locked away in a castle. Which according to Ronan isn't all that safe anyway."

Kade turned towards Ronan who had started to walk over to them when Amber had looked his way. "Who is it?"

"Deri. My people have seen him pass along information to three different clans. I have both photos and recordings if you need proof." Ronan held out a flash drive.

Kade took the device and slid it into a pocket of his jacket. "Why are you watching my people?"

"Keeping an eye on my investment." Ronan glanced towards Amber. He spun suddenly when someone entered the rooftop from the house. "What?"

"Dinner has been served." The woman bowed her head.

"Everyone make yourself at home. Please do not leave by the doors. As far as I know this place is unknown to my enemies, but why risk ruining our plans? If you need anything, see my staff." Ronan gestured towards the woman. "There are plenty of rooms if any of you wish to stay the night. It'd probably be the safest option."

"And where will you be?" Kade asked.

"Why sending missives off in every direction to try and track down Amber as I wish to meet with her tomorrow evening." Ronan grinned. "Annoying girl. She's so hard to find sometimes."

Crystal joined Amber when Ronan took to the sky. "What are you planning? Can I help?"

Amber linked arms with Crystal. "I'll tell you during dinner. I'm starving."

After dinner and numerous arguments regarding Ronan's plan, Amber and Crystal lay on one of the guest beds, looking at the pictures on Crystal's laptop.

"It took me ages to figure out what kind of hawk those feathers were from. I was looking at pictures of adult birds." Crystal clicked on the next photo. "See. The adult goshawk isn't as pretty looking as a juvenile. Which is what we are. Getting old sucks."

Amber laughed. "My grandmother often says that."

Crystal shuddered theatrically. "Please! I'm nothing like her."

Amber became serious. "How's life with Flinn?"

"Okay. He has no sense of humour. Well, he doesn't understand mine anyway. And he's so bossy. His warriors are expected to 'know their place' and I get in trouble if I'm friendly towards them. It's like they're only an extension of Flinn. No, actually they're more like property." Crystal shook her head. "I'm surprised they stay with him."

"I've figured out Gold Dragons are a bit like our movie stars."

"Yeah well, I think some of them need a good dose of reality." Crystal giggled. "But I wouldn't tell him that." She reached out to clasp Amber's hand. "Are you sure you know what you're doing?"

"Nope. But when has that ever stopped me?"

"This is life and death. It's not like wearing the wrong clothes to a party."

"I know. But this is my life. What kind of life would it be if I spent all of it hidden away?" She wasn't about to let anyone turn her into a prisoner. No matter what the reason.

"She will be protected," Rian said from the corner of the room.

Crystal pressed her hand to her heart. "I keep forgetting you're there. Make some noise occasionally, will you?"

Amber laughed. "He's got the whole unobtrusive bodyguard thing down really well, hasn't he?"

Crystal stared at Rian. "I thought you were only a bit older than us."

He nodded. "Twenty."

"Then how come you're trusted to be a bodyguard?"

"Because I've been training to be a warrior almost since birth."

Crystal turned to Amber. "You know it kind of reminded me of that time in late primary school when I slept over at your place and your brother hid under your bed."

Amber grinned. "And we didn't know he was there until we turned the lights out and he grabbed you by the ankle. I swear I'm still deaf from how loud you screamed."

"I blame him for why I can never watch a horror movie without having nightmares."

Amber laughed. "And he rushed from the room so quick Mum didn't even see him when she came to check on us. She wouldn't believe he'd been in there. She blamed it all on nightmares."

Crystal closed down her laptop, rolling onto her back to look up at the ceiling. "Are you worried about tomorrow night?"

Amber rolled over to lay beside her, putting her hands behind her head. "I'd be crazy not to be."

"Do you think it'll work?" Crystal's words were so quiet Amber had to strain to hear them.

"Ronan likes to win."

"Yeah, I guess so."

They fell silent, both lost in their own thoughts until they fell asleep. Amber's eyes opened when Rian turned the lamp off, Crystal's laptop under his arm. She smiled in thanks, surprised he smiled back at her, before she closed her eyes and returned to sleep.

Chapter Five

Amber tried to ignore the sounds she could hear around her. It was difficult though. Ronan and four Gold Warriors were hidden in the Void, keeping an eye on her as she made her way through a construction site, Rian at her heels. Maybe this wasn't such a good idea after all. Kade wasn't even close by. Since he couldn't enter the Void, he wouldn't have been able to hide his presence. But he could be there in less than five minutes. Along with Brann and Maira. Flinn had refused to be involved.

They could have called on Shannon, the Gold Dragon who would help them with the wyvern nest and who trained Jasper, but Kade didn't want to be in her debt. As it was, she was currently in his. The dragon world was so confusing sometimes, but at least thinking about it took Amber's mind off her problems. For a few seconds.

She glanced around again. As much as she dreaded meeting an assassin, she was beginning to wish one would hurry up. Just so she could complain, Amber grumbled, "Why can't Ronan ever be on time?"

"He likes to make people wait," Rian said.

"Well, it's annoying. Especially in winter. I've got better things to do than wait around here all night freezing to death."

"Patience. He will eventually arrive." Rian glanced at the watch on his arm. The band was made from dragon-leather. "About ten minutes I would say."

As if that was a cue, a man stepped out of the Void, a dagger aimed at Amber's heart. A hand grasped her arm when she tried to twist away. The next few seconds were a blur. People seemed to come from everywhere. Rian lay at her feet, the dagger protruding from his ribs as blood stained the dirt at Amber's feet. She tried to reach out to Rian but someone dragged her away from him.

Spinning with a ball of fire in her hand, she saw Ronan. "Let me go."

"We have to leave. There's more than one assassin."

"Rian–"

"Forget him. He's dying. No one can help him now. I taught him how to fight better than that."

Ronan tried to grab hold of her arm again, disappointment in his voice.

Amber pulled away and threw the ball of fire at Ronan as she did. She ignored his swearing and turned to Rian, dropping to her knees in the dirt.

His hands were pressed about the knife, his skin was ghostly pale and he finally had an expression on his face. That of pain. "Run." His word was a blood flecked whisper.

"No." Amber pulled the knife from the wound and winced at his groan of pain. All around her she heard sounds of fighting and the swoop of dragon wings. She ignored it all to press her hands against the wound the blood poured from.

"Too late," Rian murmured.

"Amber!" Ronan roared from behind her, caught in the fight.

She cleared her mind of all distractions. She'd never healed such a bad wound before, but she wasn't going to let that stop her. Rian wasn't going to die because of a knife meant for her. She felt the power pool in her hands and she concentrated on bringing to mind the books she'd read about human anatomy. She had to fix Rian before he turned dragon. She didn't know much about their anatomy. The flow of blood lessened and she felt the skin begin to knit together. Rian was barely conscious. She didn't stop healing Rian until she nearly passed out from the amount of energy she'd used.

"Amber!" Kade's voice sounded in her mind and she looked up as he flew in fast.

She guessed it had only been a few minutes she'd been working on Rian. It had seemed much longer. *"Take Rian. I can fly."* She hoped. She rose unsteadily to her feet, ignoring the blood that covered her hands and legs. A deep breath and she focused on becoming a goshawk. She was barely able to make the change and flew unsteadily upwards. A glance back showed Kade was grabbing Rian while Brann and Maira protected him from attacks. They soon joined her.

Maira swooped in front of her. *"Follow me. There's a vehicle waiting for you."*

For once Amber didn't argue. She only hoped it wouldn't be far. Two streets over Maira swooped over a black four-wheel-drive before she landed and turned human. Amber crashed into the ground, having no clue how to become human, or even how she was going to manage the couple of metres she needed to cross to the vehicle. Her problem was solved when Kade dropped Rian on the ground, became human and picked her up.

"You're an idiot," Kade said fondly as they all piled into the vehicle, Brann laying Rian in the back.

Amber unexpectedly turned human to find herself sprawled over Kade's lap, sticky blood coating her skin. "Did they get one?"

"Two."

"Anyone else hurt?" It took so much effort to stay awake, but she needed to know everyone was safe.

"One assassin died. Only minor injuries to Ronan's men. But he wants to see you. Immediately."

Relief hit as exhaustion swamped her. "Not now," Amber murmured as she snuggled against Kade's chest and fell asleep.

* * *

Amber woke to Ronan standing over her, glaring. She looked behind him and recognised the walls of the bedroom in his house.

"You didn't stick to the plan."

"If the plan was to let Rian die, it sucked."

"You agreed to it. The plan was to keep you safe at all costs."

"I didn't think you'd leave Rian there." Amber struggled to sit up and waved Ronan back when he held out a hand to her. "How many sons have you got that you can throw their lives away like that?"

"I can have more. Hopefully ones that won't fail me. You should have told me you could heal."

"Where's Rian?" Amber looked to the corner Ronan pointed in. She frowned. "Should you be up and about? You almost died last night."

"I am well enough to guard you."

"Didn't you tell me healing wasn't one of your abilities?"

Amber turned back to Ronan. "Didn't you tell me it could take years for all my abilities to develop?"

"Are you expecting me to believe you didn't have that power when I asked you?"

Amber swung her legs out of the bed and grimaced. The sheets were stained from her blood streaked pants. Only her hands and arms had been cleaned. "I don't care what you believe." Her legs buckled as she slid out of bed and she was grateful Rian moved forward to support her. He stepped back into his corner as soon as she was steady.

Ronan's eyes narrowed as he looked from Amber to Rian. "I believe it's time for you to go home, boy. Hound can take over your duties here. You failed last night."

"No he didn't. He saved my life. What else was he meant to do? Die?"

"He put you at risk by getting injured. You wouldn't leave like you were supposed to and he nearly caused me to break my word. That is unforgivable."

Rian came out of the corner he stood in and knelt at Amber's feet, pressing his arms and upper body against the carpeted floor.

"Get up!" Ronan roared. "Get up you traitor."

When Ronan started towards Rian, Amber stepped up to him, forcing herself to meet his angry gaze. She reached out with her mind for Kade and called him to her. "Leave Rian alone."

"He isn't yours. He's mine and I can do what I want with him."

Amber looked down at Rian who watched her. *"I don't understand what you're asking me."*

"He swore not to harm you or yours."

Amber looked back into Ronan's pale blue eyes. "No, he's mine."

"You can't afford to keep a warrior. Do you have fifty thousand a year to give him, plus bonuses for any battles he fights on your behalf?"

Kade stepped inside the room. "She earns more than that a year as my mage."

She did? Amber tried not to show her surprise. She certainly wasn't going to argue it right this minute. "He's mine." She continued to meet Ronan's gaze.

"You'll regret this."

"No I won't. Because after you calm down, I'm sure you'll come up with some convoluted reason why I owe you for this."

"Amber, be careful. He's not a good man to owe." Kade came to her side. *"And touch Rian on the shoulder so he can rise and know you've accepted his services."*

Amber did as Kade directed and Rian rose to stand at her back. "I think you're taking this the wrong way."

"You've stolen one of my warriors. What other way can I take it?"

Rian spoke before Amber could think of a reply. "I owe her a life. As your warrior, that debt would be yours."

"I gave you life long before she ever did." Ronan glared at his son.

"And last night you discarded it. Amber chose to pick it up and save it. I owe her a life debt. Do you wish to pay it?"

Silence filled the room until Ronan growled. "I always said you'd never amount to anything. All you've ever done is cause me problems." He turned to

Amber. "And I will collect the debt you owe me for this."

"It is only a small debt," Rian said.

Ronan once again stared at Rian before he gave a sharp nod and left the room.

With a deep breath of relief, Amber sank onto the bed and stared up at Rian. "What am I meant to do with you?"

Rian grinned fleetingly. "Nothing. I am meant to serve you."

"This is too complicated."

Kade sat beside her. "Things tend to get that way around you."

"What next?"

"We need to find out if you having your own warrior means you can't help clean out a wyvern nest with us."

"Oh, you'd just love that, wouldn't you?" Amber looked from Rian to Kade. "This wasn't something you hatched between you, was it?"

"I will contact them and assure them I will only be at your side to protect you due to assassination attempts. I will not interfere in the test in any way," Rian said. "If helping clean out the wyvern nest is what you wish to do I will do everything possible other than leave you unprotected to ensure you can have your wish." He turned to Kade. "Will you be able to watch over Amber while I look into the matter?"

Kade nodded and Rian left the room. Amber stared after him frowning. "Why do I feel like I just missed something?"

"You know how you complain about how Maira and Brann have to follow my every wish?" When Amber nodded, Kade grinned. "Well, that's exactly what you now have with Rian."

"No."

Kade's grin became a laugh.

"Oh shut up. This is terrible. I don't want that kind of blind obedience."

"It won't be completely blind. He just finished telling you the only time he'd ignore your wishes is when they put you at risk."

Amber shook her head. "I didn't hear that."

Before Kade could explain, Crystal burst into her room and threw her arms around her. "Thank god you're okay. When they brought you in last night, covered in blood, I nearly had a heart attack. So did your brother." Crystal pulled back to look Amber over. "Are you sure you're okay? You're not hurt?"

"It was all Rian's blood."

"That's what they said, but," Crystal smiled wryly.

"You know me. I couldn't stop thinking of all the most terrible things possible. It was worse than a horror movie."

"I'm good. The only thing wrong with me is I'm starving."

"Then let's get you something to eat." Crystal dragged Amber off the bed.

Amber looked down at herself with a grimace. "After I've had a wash."

Crystal wrinkled her nose. "That'd probably be best. You're a mess."

"Gee, thanks."

Crystal grinned. "Any time."

Chapter Six

Amber slid out of the saddle Kade wore. She started to remove it so he could turn back to human form, but Rian beat her to the job. She still felt slightly queasy from slipping through the Void, with the help of some Gold Warriors, to reach the dragon lands so she didn't argue with him that she could do it. Instead, she turned to stare at the castle that rose above them, set in an impossibly green land. This was a little castle? She couldn't imagine how much space a big one would take up.

Crystal came to stand beside Amber, linking her arm through Amber's. "We're going to stay there?"

Amber could only nod as she stared in awe at the stone building that towered over them, turrets at each corner.

"This is going to kill me not to be able to brag about it when I go back to school."

"Hey." They both turned to face Maira who snapped their twin expressions of disbelief. She grinned. "Brag away. Just tell them it was in Europe."

"Don't you dare show anyone that photo. I must look a mess." Crystal marched over to Maira and tried to take the phone from her.

Rian stopped in front of Amber, her luggage in his hands. "I will put your things in your room if you stay with Kade."

Amber nodded. She'd felt awkward with Rian since accepting him as her warrior yesterday. It just didn't feel right. Her gaze sought out Kade and she watched as he strode towards her, a grin on his face.

"What do you think?"

Amber shrugged, trying to look unimpressed. "Who normally lives here?"

Kade slung an arm around her shoulders. "This is where I was raised."

"Your family live here?"

Kade shook his head. "No. When I was a few years old my parents sent me to live here. They were in the middle of a war and thought it was safer to leave me in a place no one would find me."

"Who looked after you?"

"The place was full of people. There were plenty to look after me."

"Didn't you miss your family?"

"They visited often." Kade grinned. "Quit frowning. I'm not emotionally scarred from my childhood. I loved living here."

Maira joined them. "In other words, he had a castle full of servants at his beck and call whose only thought was to cater to his every wish."

Amber shook her head, still trying to grasp the idea of growing up in a castle. "It's so big."

Kade linked his fingers through hers. "Come and I'll show you around. There are also some people I want you to meet."

By the time Kade had shown her the main rooms, introduced her to some of the staff who'd been there since he was a toddler and left her in her room, which was next to his, Amber felt lost and confused. Rian stood by the door, guarding her as usual and she guessed that somewhere two Gold Dragons took turns to hide in the Void and watch her every move. She could only think that they must be extremely bored.

Glancing around the bedroom, her gaze was drawn to the four poster bed with dark red velvet drapes. The curtains at the windows matched the bed and the armchairs in one corner of the room were also covered with the same fabric. All the furniture looked antique, with a dark timber duchess, a small table near the group of armchairs and a wardrobe making up the rest of the furniture. As luxurious as it all was, Amber wanted to go home. This place wasn't her.

Crystal burst into her room. "Isn't it insane? I swear I'm never leaving this place. I feel like a princess."

Amber tried to return Crystal's smile.

"Uh oh." Crystal grinned even more. "Too many changes, huh?"

Amber laughed. Crystal knew her too well.

"Well, I love it here. And I want one."

"You and every Gold Dragon," Rian said.

Crystal frowned. "But I thought it was land they wanted."

"And to protect your lands you need some kind of fortification on it."

Crystal stared at Rian. "You mean that when we talk about getting Ronan's lands back for him we're actually talking about getting him a castle?"

Rian nodded.

"Ohh! How unfair. I want my own castle too."

"That is one of the tests for Gold Dragons."

Crystal grinned at Rian's words. "I've got to find Flinn. I want to know how long before we get our castle."

Amber laughed as Crystal rushed out of the room. She felt a little better, but not much.

"Do you want your own castle too?"

She turned towards Rian, thinking about his question. She eventually shook her head. "I just want to be left in peace. I think a castle would have even more people after us."

"There is no peace in our lands. We are perpetually at war with each other. Allies one day, could be enemies who stab you in the back the next day."

"Do you say that because you've been raised by Ronan?"

Rian shook his head. "We are all like that. Ronan is fairly typical of our people. A little more harsh than some."

"And you?"

"I was raised on war." He paused. "War, deceit and loyalty to only one man. But eventually, like his other sons, I have learned the only loyalty Ronan has is to himself."

"I'm sorry."

Rian shrugged. "Our world is different. And Ronan came from an even harsher time in our history. We learn to adapt and most of us thrive on the way things are."

"You don't?"

"Peace is a dream for dragons who have long gone grey and are nearing the end. Death is the only true peace to be found in our lands."

Amber shivered at his words. She wanted to go home more than ever. But where was home? Her grandmother's place? The house she was raised in? She was starting to think she didn't fit in either of those places. She spun as the door opened again and her racing heart slowed when she saw it was Kade.

"You're safe here." Kade reached out and took her hand.

"Am I? What about the one passing information?"

"He's being watched and we'll track him back to those he's dealing with."

Amber pulled away from Kade, wandering across the room to look out the narrow window. The land looked beautiful, but she wondered how much blood had been spilled so Kade's family could own it. After witnessing the fight two nights ago, it had become clear to her exactly what taking Ronan's lands back would involve. She felt Kade behind her.

"What's bothering you, Amber?"

She looked over her shoulder at him. "Do you expect me to kill when we help Ronan get his lands back?"

Kade wrapped his arms around her. "I expect only

what you're capable of. But remember, you are part of the agreement. If you refuse to help him get his lands, things will be back to the way they started."

"Ronan would be worse than an assassin after you," Rian said softly.

Amber guessed he'd know since he'd been raised by the man. She turned in Kade's arms. "What should I do?"

"Let's figure out who's trying to kill you and deal with the wyvern nest. We can worry about Ronan later."

"Ronan often says, keep your friends close and your enemies even closer," Rian said to Amber alone.

"Is he my enemy?" She turned so she could see Rian's face. As usual, it was expressionless.

"He has no true friends."

Amber felt a sense of dread at Rian's words. She couldn't afford more enemies. She had to do something. And offending him yesterday probably hadn't been a good idea. Nor throwing a fireball at him the day before. Amber sighed. What could she do? How was she going to deal with this world of war and deceit when she only wanted peace? Well, she didn't expect total peace, but she certainly didn't want an assassin hiding behind every bush. There had to be a way to get what she wanted. She couldn't live the rest of her life hunted.

"How about lunch? Forget everything for now and come and eat. My people have prepared a feast."

Amber nodded. Although she did wonder how it would be possible to eat with all the knots in her stomach.

* * *

Amber paced back and forth in her room. She stopped and stared at her phone, for probably the hundredth time. After a glance at Rian in the corner, she began to pace again. This was getting her nowhere. She had to make up her mind. And fast. Too long and it'd look like she was running scared. She might be, but she didn't want anyone else to know. A decision had to be made and from all she'd learned during lunch, it was just like in her own world. The clan with the most power and biggest army was left alone by those weaker. The aim was to be at the top of the ladder.

There was one thing she could be certain of. Ronan kept his word. If she kept hers, then he'd be the one ally she could be certain of. Which was a rare thing amongst dragons. Dropping onto her bed, she dialled

Ronan's number before she could talk herself out of ringing.

"What do you want?"

His tone didn't promise a pleasant conversation. She needed to find a way to change that. "Why good evening, Ronan. Yes, it is lovely weather we're having."

"Oh, so we're using manners tonight are we?"

Amber smiled, knowing he'd hear it in her voice. That hadn't worked as well as she'd hoped. "Well, it's so lovely here I just can't help but be in a good mood."

"Was there a reason for your call?"

"Of course there was. All the drama while I was visiting you completely made me forget. I turn seventeen in ten days." She tried not to think about what had happened during her visit, but the sight of a dagger stuck in Rian was still clear in her mind.

"Good for you. Ring me then and I'll try and remember to wish you a happy birthday."

Amber laughed, trying to keep her worries from colouring the tone of her voice. "I was actually hoping you'd come to my party." Her smile grew wider when there was silence on the other end of the phone. Maybe he was thinking about it.

"Why?"

Her heart plummeted. Obviously, he wasn't. "What do you mean why?" She struggled to think of a logical reason other than she was terrified that she'd turned him into an enemy. None came to mind.

"Why would you invite me to your party?"

"I've invited all my friends. Well, the non-human ones anyway."

"Try again, Amber. Why are you inviting me to your party?"

Still no answer came to mind. "Because you're actually kind of likeable when you're not being a bastard."

"I thought I was one all the time."

"Oh, you have your fleeting moments where you either forget or you actually let your nice side out to play."

Ronan snorted in disbelief. "I don't have a nice side. Why don't you ask Rian?"

"I've already talked to Rian about you." Maybe sidetracking him would make him forget he wanted to know why she'd invited him. Or at least give her time to come up with a reason. She hadn't expected him to demand why.

"And what did he have to say?"

"That you're extremely loyal."

"Try again. I'm not buying that one either."

Amber laughed, still playing for time. "To yourself."

"Much better."

"So, are you going to come to my party?"

"What are you planning?"

"Food, music, dancing."

"And what else?"

"Ronan, I'm not planning anything to harm you. Why would I?"

"But you are after something. Don't tell me you're hoping to be friends." The last word was said like it was poison. "Not after you stole my son."

"Of course not. I was told you don't have friends. So maybe we can just be sociable enemies."

"I will get to the bottom of this. I'll ring you back shortly."

Amber stared at the phone in her hand and wondered what he planned to do. She looked over at Rian.

"He is going to ring his Gold Dragons to see what they have to say."

Amber nodded. She'd guessed they'd report everything to Ronan. Her phone rang and she nearly dropped it. She took a deep breath when she saw Ronan's name on the display.

"That was quick. Did they have anything

interesting to tell you?" There was no way she was going to let him know how worried she was.

"I won't let you out of the deal. You will help me get my lands back or you and yours will die."

It took all her willpower to keep her tone even and not beg him to leave her friends and family alone. "That part isn't the problem. It just hit me earlier that I wouldn't be able to kill anyone so I wondered how much use I'd be."

"What's your game?"

"Honestly?"

"That would be a change."

It was probably too soon to tell him that he was the only ally she was certain of. A pity she'd failed at coming up with a valid reason. "I have no idea. But it didn't seem right you were the only one who hadn't been invited." When the silence stretched out, Amber asked, "Are you still there?"

"Unity. You're right. I do need to be there. People need to see me linked with you. There might be hope for you after all."

"God forbid." Amber smiled as she said the words, relieved he'd created a plausible reason for her.

"Give it a century and you might even be able to compete with me, but I doubt it."

She shuddered at the thought of living that long

and quickly put it from her mind. It was too much to cope with. "I'll see you at my party." She looked up as Kade entered the room.

"Send me an invite." Ronan disconnected.

"What have you done now, Amber?"

She smiled at Kade as she rose to her feet. She was actually feeling a little more in control of her life after that call. "Send Ronan an invite."

Kade stared at her. "I hope you know what you're doing."

She held her smile in place, refusing to answer since she didn't know how many listened in. She wondered what Rian told Kade when he glanced in that direction and nodded. What did it matter? She could find out later. Right now she had other matters to deal with. Her smile disappeared. "What's with the separate rooms?"

"What?"

"Why did you put me in a room next to yours?"

Kade looked confused. "You want to share my room? Don't you always complain that you never have enough space?"

Amber shrugged. "I've kind of got used to you there each night." When Kade smiled, Amber jabbed a finger at his chest. "But don't go getting any ideas."

Kade laughed. "Too late. I've been having ideas for months."

Amber bit back a smile as she pushed past him. "Then make sure you continue to keep them to yourself." She strode to Kade's room and flung open the door. It was very similar to the room she'd been given except it was done in navy velvet. It wasn't home, but it would do. For now.

Chapter Seven

Amber was woken by whispering at the door. She stretched and realised the bed was empty. Well, other than her of course. Leaning up on an elbow, she tried to look past Rian to see who was at the door. When that failed, she strained to hear. "Let her in," she mumbled and then drew a pillow over her face. It had taken her ages to fall asleep last night. Too many worries and a completely different environment. She held on tight to her pillow as someone tried to pull it away from her.

"Come on, Amber. I'm starving. Let's go have breakfast," Crystal pleaded.

"Sleeping."

"Then why did you let me into your room?"

"To tell you to go away." She rolled over onto her stomach when Crystal succeeded in taking the pillow from her.

"You're missing an amazing day. Come on." Crystal shook Amber.

"Ronan's coming to my party."

Crystal stopped shaking her. "What! Why?"

"Because I invited him."

"Get up and tell me what you're going on about. Are you sure you didn't dream that?"

Amber rolled back over and smiled at Crystal. "Nope."

"Doesn't he have enough people watching you without needing to do the job himself? He's got two in your bedroom right now."

Amber glanced around her room and saw only Rian. And he wasn't Ronan's anymore. "Rian is my warrior."

"Okay. Fine. But the other one is his." Crystal gestured towards the window.

Amber's bedroom door burst open again and Flinn strode in. "I've been looking everywhere for you. Why didn't you answer me when I called?"

Crystal gestured over her shoulder for him to wait a moment as she addressed the window. "Of course I can see you. You're standing right there near the window." She turned to face Flinn. "And I didn't answer because I'm not a dog. Don't call me like I'm one."

Amber slid out of bed and walked towards her window. No one was there. She turned to face Crystal. "Forget about Flinn for a minute. What do you mean someone's at the window?" Amber half screamed as a man appeared at her window. She jumped back from him, Rian immediately at her side, steadying her.

"You are safe. This is Chait, one of Ronan's Golds," Rian assured her.

"But he's been there the entire time." Crystal looked around at everyone with bewilderment in her eyes.

"You can see into the Void?" Chait took a step towards Crystal.

"I can?" Crystal looked towards Amber.

She shrugged. "I didn't see him until just a moment ago."

"About time you finally figured out what else you can do," Flinn said.

Crystal grinned and grabbed hold of Amber's hands. "I can see into the Void."

Amber returned her best friend's grin. "It looks that way."

Crystal squealed and spun Amber around in a half dance, half excited bounce. "I can see into the Void!"

"In that case you can come and check my room. I

could have sworn there was someone in there earlier," Flinn said. "And you also need to do some practice. This isn't a holiday you know."

Amber and Crystal glanced at Flinn, then at each other before bursting into laughter. They ignored his growl as they spun around one more time.

"This is so exciting." Crystal turned to Chait, who was still near the window. "Can you go back into the Void again?" She waited a moment then added, "Please?"

"He already has," Amber said.

Crystal giggled. "Not for me he hasn't." She frowned. "You know this is going to be difficult. How am I going to figure out if a person is here or in the Void? There has to be some way of telling the difference." Crystal looked towards the window again. "Can I borrow you to practice on?" She frowned. "Why not?" She glanced towards Amber. "Oh, of course." She turned to Flinn. "Why can't you enter the Void yet? Can you find me someone who can?"

Flinn looked like he was ready to explode. "Practice first and then you can play with your new ability."

Crystal poked her tongue out at Flinn as she danced across the room. "Spoil sport." She linked her arm through his and Flinn started to pull away.

"You're not frightened of me are you?" She grinned up at him as he froze in mid motion. "Come on. Let's go and practice so I can get to the fun stuff." She started for the door, Flinn forced into step beside her. "But I need to grab something to eat on the way or I might pass out from hunger."

Amber smiled slightly as she watched her friend disappear. So much for breakfast together. The smile widened into a grin. But at least Crystal now had another ability. They needed to find out what else Jay could do other than throw balls of fire. Amber wondered if he'd have her ability to heal too.

She grabbed a change of clothes and headed for the bathroom, wishing she'd asked Crystal to check it was clear before she went in. Although Ronan had agreed the Gold Dragons wouldn't follow her in there, she didn't completely trust him. No one did. She wondered if his Gold was ringing him right now to let him know about Crystal's new ability. She guessed he probably was, but she couldn't be sure. Although, she was certain of one thing. The information would be better if it came from her.

After a hurried shower, Amber returned to the bedroom to ring Ronan. He answered almost immediately.

"I've heard from you two days in a row. Should I feel privileged?"

"Of course you should," Amber said with a laugh, refusing to let his caustic words bother her.

"You're probably wasting your time with this call. We're never going to be friends."

"Didn't you once tell me we'd be friends before your lands were captured?"

"I only meant that you would be my friend, not that I'd be yours. But that was before you stole my son."

"Nah, I took a burden from you. Isn't that what friends are for?" She had to figure out a way to make him okay with that. She didn't regret saving Rian, but she was worried about the problems it was going to cause her with Ronan.

"Is there a point to this conversation, Amber?"

"Yeah. I wanted to tell you Crystal discovered a new ability."

"I already know."

"You've got to be kidding. Did he ring you while it was being discovered?"

"No. While you were taking a shower."

"Huh. I was barely five minutes."

"Then I guess you need to be a little faster in future."

"Or not bother since you've got so many people reporting to you." That comment should help her out next time she didn't tell him something. It was the perfect excuse to fall back on.

"You're starting to annoy me, Amber."

"My mum says that to me a lot. I guess you're rethinking your views on humans and how fascinating we are too, but I finally figured something out while I was trying to sleep last night."

After a moment of silence, Ronan asked, "Are you planning to tell me or are you going to hang up and let me get on with my day?"

She considered hanging up, but decided she would tell him after all. "In some ways we're a lot alike. You don't like change either. And yet when things stay the same they bore you. You also put people in boxes and you don't like it when they change boxes. But most of all, you like to be in control."

"I am nothing like you." Ronan disconnected.

Amber sighed. Maybe she'd gone too far this time. She looked over to see Rian watched her. Glancing around the room she wondered where the Gold Dragon was. Maybe it was time for breakfast. Unless of course she'd upset Ronan so much he'd finally break one of his promises and help the assassins that were after her. Amber pushed her phone into a pocket of her jacket and stepped out of Kade's room. How the hell was she going to fix the mess she'd just made? And fix it without seeming to back pedal. She should've waited until she was a lot more awake. And had slept properly. He might not go against his word and harm her, but he could make life difficult and she had enough problems without adding more. There had to be some way to fix the problems that had been increasing between them since she'd taken Rian from him.

"Do you need me to show you where to find something?"

Amber looked over her shoulder to where Rian stood, waiting for her to step out of the doorway. "Yeah. I'd probably get lost trying to find the dining room."

She quietly followed Rian, her mind turning over what she could do next, but she knew her words were true. Ronan hated change too. And he always wanted to be in control. Always.

* * *

Amber found out just how mad she'd made Ronan when she went for a walk with Rian later. Ronan appeared on the path in front of her, sitting on a boulder. One leg was drawn up in front of him, his hand resting on his knee, a gun held loosely.

"Did you miss me that much?" She waved Rian back when he stepped between her and his father. "He won't hurt me. We still have a lot to do together."

"You heard her, boy. Get out of the way."

Rian hesitated and Amber grew worried Ronan might actually break his word and harm his son. After all, Rian was of no use to him now he was no longer his. *"Give us space. We need to talk."* Rian nodded once and moved away. He kept her in sight but gave her plenty of privacy.

"Do I take it you've chased away your Gold as well?" Amber asked.

Ronan rose to his feet and tucked his gun in the back of his dragon-leather pants. "That's none of your concern."

Amber smiled, determined to keep him off balance while she figured out a way to repair the damage she'd caused not only earlier today, but also when she'd accepted Rian as her warrior. Somehow she had to manage it without taking back anything she'd said or done. "I'm such a fearsome creature I guess you should keep him nearby."

"You're going to get yourself killed one day by saying the wrong thing." Ronan turned away from her and started to walk along the path she'd been following.

Amber fell into step beside him. "Probably. It seems to be one of my failings."

"That doesn't bother you?"

Looking up at him, she smiled. "Does it bother you?" She wasn't about to go back on what she'd said.

Ronan stopped and stared down at her. "Does what bother me?"

"That you tend to do the same thing. Do you do it for the same reason I do, or has it just become a habit over the centuries?"

"Are you deliberately trying to annoy me?"

Amber shook her head. "No. I've decided I might as well be honest with you. I'm shadowed by so many of your people it isn't worth the effort trying to lie. I'd end up tripping over a lie somewhere along the way. And do you know, I actually like not having to watch what I say to you." She grinned, reminding herself to breathe as she waited to see how he took her words. "It's kind of fun."

"Fun."

She chuckled when she heard the tone of disgust in his voice. But at least he wasn't angry and there was an expression in his eyes that she thought might even be curiosity. "Yeah. You should try it sometime. It might be a nice change from all the layers of lies and plots you usually wallow in. Oops, but I forgot. You don't like change."

"You seriously expect me to believe you plan only to tell me the truth."

"Of course I don't think you're going to believe me." Amber laughed, trying to keep her tone light. She could do this. She had no choice. Somehow she had to prevent Ronan from becoming her enemy. "That's actually half the fun." She was again tempted to tell him that their agreement meant he was the only ally she could really trust, but she still didn't think it was the right time. Maybe it never would be.

Ronan reached out and grabbed hold of her chin to tilt her head back further. "Are you telling me you're making a vow to only tell me the truth?"

"No. I'm telling you I don't plan to lie to you. You'd find out anyway."

"Are you saying you've never lied to me?"

Amber couldn't resist smiling. "Of course not."

"What have you lied about?"

"I'm not sure. But I know there must have been a few things. Like when you asked me to heal Rian when you kidnapped me."

Ronan let her go. "You could have healed him."

She nodded.

"What else?"

"I don't know. Ask me a question."

"Will you kill when you help take my lands?"

"I don't think I'll be able to, but then who knows what will happen when everything is going crazy during battle?"

"You will keep your speculations about me to yourself."

"Were they too accurate?" It was an effort, but Amber managed to prevent herself from smiling. That wouldn't have helped her repair the damage she'd caused.

"No."

"Okay." Her tone said she felt anything but belief in his protest.

"I mean it, Amber."

"I know. But then I never know when I'm alone or not. You've always got people hiding in the Void as they watch me."

"None of my people will hear you in the bathroom. If you have water running, and you need their help, you better scream loud as it interferes with a dragon's sense of hearing." Ronan stared intently at her. "What is your game?"

Maybe it was time to tell him after all. "It's pointless to stay enemies with you. You're probably one of the few people I can actually trust."

"And how did you arrive at that conclusion?"

"Because everyone says you never break your word and that's why you rarely give it. That it's more than just a law to you."

"And what is your word worth?"

"I really like the idea of people's words having value. It's kind of old fashioned to my world, but I like it anyway."

"Breaking one's word is a killing offence in my world. That's one reason why you must word things very carefully and make sure you abide by them."

Amber nodded. "And yet you gave us a lot of power over you with your vow."

Ronan shrugged. "I only gave the power to you. It ends at your death. You will gain enemies. You already have."

"All I'll have to do is run to you and your vow means you'll have to protect me. Because to do otherwise would be to let me come to harm."

"If you made it to me in time."

"It's kind of like having an uncle to watch out for me. I won't say like having another father because that role has never suited you. Let's hope you make a better uncle."

Ronan stared at her intently. "Has anyone ever told you that you're very odd?"

"Quite a few times." Amber smiled fleetingly, a little more easy about Ronan's intentions. It was probably past time to change the subject before she ruined all the progress she'd made. "Have you learned anything from your captives?"

"Only that they must enjoy pain."

Amber screwed up her face. "Please. I don't want to hear the gory stuff." She bit back the words she really wanted to say, knowing that no matter what she said, he'd continue to treat his captives however he wanted.

"See, we're nothing alike."

Amber met his ancient, pale blue eyes. "Did you like hearing about torture when you were nearly seventeen?"

"That was centuries ago. As if I'd remember."

"I think you do." She had probably pushed him far enough for one day. Smiling, she linked her arm through Ronan's, ignoring his fleeting look of surprise. "Enough with stress and drama. I was taking a walk to leave all that behind. Since you chased Rian away, how about you tell me the names of the plants I point out to you. Everything is so different here." She was amazed when Ronan fell into step beside her, but she made sure she didn't show it. "That one. What is it? I love the colour of its flowers."

Chapter Eight

Amber pushed away from Kade as she tried to answer her phone. She swatted his hands out of the way while she looked at the display.

"Hello, Ronan."

"What are you doing right now?"

"Making out with Kade."

"Do you really think I want to hear that?"

"Then why did you ask me what I was doing?"

Ronan sighed. "Are you busy?"

Amber laughed. "Didn't I just say I was?"

"Amber! You're trying my patience."

"Then why don't you ask me what you really want to know?"

"The assassin that is still alive says he'll only talk to you."

Amber frowned. "Still alive?"

"The other one died. When can you get here?"

She thought it best not to ask for more details on the dead assassin. There were some things she was probably better off not knowing. For the sake of her sanity. "We had planned to make an attack on the wyvern nest tomorrow morning."

"Then you better get over here tonight."

Amber stifled a yawn. "I'm already in bed."

"Do you really think that matters to me?"

Amber sighed. "Okay. I'll be there as soon as possible. But if I fall off Kade mid-flight tomorrow morning due to lack of sleep it's your fault."

"Strap yourself in properly and it won't be an issue. And bring Crystal with you. I don't know if this is a trap. I won't have anyone in the Void. If she sees anyone in it, they aren't mine. As far as I know, no one knows about the location of this house, but complacency leads to death." Ronan hung up before Amber could reply.

She sighed as she dropped back on the bed to stare up at the canopy of Kade's bed. "So much for an early night."

"Don't complain to me. I tried to stop you from answering the phone."

Amber ignored Kade and rolled out of bed, taking the leather pants and jacket Rian held out for her. "Thanks."

"I have contacted Orin so he can inform Flinn and Crystal," Rian said.

"Why didn't you just let Crystal know?" Amber asked.

"As I am your first warrior, I notify Flinn's first warrior. It is inappropriate for me to directly contact Flinn or Crystal except in extreme circumstances."

Amber grinned. "You're my only warrior. And I'm sure it would have been much more fun to horrify Flinn by contacting Crystal."

"You will have to learn the proper way to do things eventually. People have died from giving smaller insults."

"That would be an insult?" Amber stared at Rian. "Seriously?" She shook her head when he nodded. "You people are warped."

Kade grabbed her around the waist and pulled her back against him. "Extremely warped. Now stop trying to stir everyone. For someone who says they like peace you certainly stir up a lot of trouble."

"I'm just joking around. Doesn't anyone have a sense of humour these days?" She turned in his arms to look up at him.

"No." He dropped a light kiss on her lips. "Now go and get dressed."

They were ready within twenty minutes and

Amber steeled herself to pass through the Void, with the help of the Gold Dragons Kade had organised to take them through. Neither he nor Flinn had learned how to travel through the Void yet, even though they'd both held a Pliethin.

Amber, Kade, Rian, Brann, Crystal, Flinn and Orin travelled to Ronan's home. The rest, and that reluctantly included Jasper, stayed behind to cover for them. Shannon, Jasper's Gold Dragon, was in residence with her two warriors to help take the wyvern nest tomorrow morning. Dragons were a secretive bunch, even with their allies.

"I hope this isn't going to take all night," Flinn said as he landed on Ronan's rooftop garden and became human.

"Then I suggest getting on with it instead of standing around socialising," Ronan snapped.

Amber strode to Ronan's side and linked her arm with his as she headed for the house entrance. "And here I thought we'd have time to sit and gossip over tea and scones."

"We're not going through the let's be friends crap again, are we?" Ronan asked.

Amber smiled up at him, almost certain that he wasn't as cranky as he sounded. "But I'm just so lovable you won't be able to resist being my friend."

"Friends are enemies who haven't got around to stabbing you in the back yet."

"That's a sad way of looking at life." Amber shook her head slowly.

"It's realistic."

"Sad."

Ronan pulled away from Amber. "Enough." He turned towards Crystal, who along with everyone else had followed them inside. "You shouldn't see a single person. The house is empty apart from the prisoner. All my warriors are outside."

Crystal nodded and started forward, Orin a step in front of her. Amber fell into step beside her, linking her arm with Crystal.

"I think your ability is so much more useful than mine," Amber complained.

"At least you can prevent people from dying," Crystal said.

"Yeah but you can see attacks before they come out of the Void at you."

"Don't you ever shut up?" Ronan asked from behind them.

Amber grinned at him over her shoulder. "Sure I do. When I'm sleeping."

Ronan ignored her. "Turn left up here. It's the third door on the right."

Crystal nodded, her gaze darting everywhere as she walked. "It all looks clear so far."

Amber really wished Ronan hadn't interrupted her conversation with Crystal. Now she was left to think about what might be waiting for her. Was this a trap? And why her? Why couldn't the assassin have told Ronan instead of her? Maybe Ronan's cynicism was rubbing off on her, but she couldn't think of one good reason why the assassin wanted to see her. Only really bad scenarios came to mind. Ones filled with blood and dying.

Orin opened the door for Crystal and, stepping into the room, moved to the right. Crystal glanced around. "Only one person." She entered so everyone else could follow.

Amber managed to enter last, uncertain if she really wanted to hear anything an assassin might want to tell her. She stopped. A man wearing dragon-leather pants was chained to a metal stool that was bolted to the floor. Water dripped from his body onto a recently mopped floor and he stared at her out of one green eye, the other swollen shut. His body and face were covered in bruises and cuts, several still oozing blood to mingle with the water droplets. Amber fought the urge to reach out and heal him.

"Only her." The man's voice was surprisingly strong considering his condition.

"That wasn't the deal. I agreed to bring her here." Ronan drew back a fist.

"No." Amber raced between the prisoner and Ronan. "Please. No more."

Ronan stared down at her, anger radiating from him. "Don't be weak, Amber."

"I'll see him with just Crystal and my bodyguard." She held his glare with one of her own. "The three of us are more than enough for anything he might try. If he can try anything in this state."

Ronan remained silent then nodded sharply. When Flinn opened his mouth to argue, he turned his glare on him. Flinn instantly shut his mouth. "Everyone out." His voice brooked no argument. He paused in the doorway to face them. "No one can hear what happens in this room once the door is closed."

Amber suppressed a flare of fear and nodded calmly. She watched as Ronan quietly closed the door. Forcing herself to breathe evenly, she turned to face the man. "Why did you wish to see me?"

"When you first saw me, what did you think of?"

"What?"

"When you entered this room and looked at me. I want to know what your expression meant."

"I wanted to heal you."

"Why are you allied with Ronan?"

"Why did you want to see me?"

"Humour me. He's not going to let me live, so what's the harm?"

Ronan would kill this man because he'd tried to kill her. He wasn't the one who'd stabbed Rian, but he could have been. She should want him dead, but she didn't. "What's your name?"

"Daray."

"What did you want to tell me?"

"I wish to ask a favour of you."

"I thought you had information you'd tell only me."

Rian stood by the door, his arms crossed. "I think it is time to leave. He has nothing of importance to say."

"I want to go too," Crystal said from beside Amber.

"Please. My parents were renegades. I wanted better for my daughter. I thought this was that chance. Not once has your name been linked with Ronan. Most of us would have known better than to bother. Take my daughter into your care and I'll give you all the information you need."

"Oh no," Crystal wailed, grasping Amber's arm.

"We can't let Ronan kill him. Who'll look after his daughter?"

"I think Crystal needs to leave the room," Rian said directly to Amber.

"But–"

"Do you need to leave as well and let me deal with this?" Rian interrupted her.

She sighed. "Crystal. Let them know not to disturb me and there's no need for you to return. Rian will be enough."

"But Amber–"

Amber shook her head. "Crystal." She met her friend's gaze. *"I need to focus on what both Rian and Daray have to say. This is important."*

Crystal hugged Amber tightly. *"Don't do anything stupid."*

Amber grinned as Crystal let her go. "I thought that was a given."

Crystal laughed. "Just don't." She walked towards the door, a single glance over her shoulder before she left.

Amber turned to face Daray the moment the door closed. She couldn't help herself. She reached out and took some of the wounds from his face. The swell from his eye, the cut from his lip and mended his broken nose.

"Why?"

Amber pondered Daray's question and then shrugged. "I'm a healer I guess."

"Ronan will not give you all night to make your deal. Tell us what information you have and we will decide what value it has," Rian said.

Daray shook his head. "You could easily say it was valueless. I recognise you for his son. Now I'm looking into your eyes." He turned his gaze to Amber. "Please swear you'll see to my daughter if I give you this information."

"What do you expect us to do for your daughter? Are there other family who would believe they should have a part in her life and what is her age? Where is she at this moment and what current plans did you have in place for her if something should happen to you?" Rian came closer, his hands clasped behind his back as he studied Daray.

"Does he speak for you?" Daray looked at Amber, but nodded towards Rian.

"He's my bodyguard. He takes the position very seriously." She couldn't resist smiling at the understatement.

"I am her first warrior and I owe her a life. I will not let her do anything that puts her life in jeopardy."

Daray nodded. "My daughter, Doneele, is thirteen.

A woman she calls Granny has cared for her since her mother died years ago. Her mother was a renegade too. She's my only child still surviving. And she's Gold."

"The best we could offer her is to become a warrior. We cannot guarantee to sponsor her so she can become a Gold Warrior."

"But her children or even her children's children may no longer have the stigma of renegade attached to them and can make alliances that will allow them to become Gold Warriors. I just want to give her a chance to avoid being a renegade. Being born one usually means you are one forever, regardless of how much Gold is in your bloodline."

Amber looked towards Rian. *"What should I do? I don't want the kid to suffer because of her parents. You know how all this stuff works better than me."*

"Amber offers you this. If you willingly give all the information you know, and it is of reasonable value, she will see your daughter is cared for, trained as a warrior and placed with a Gold Dragon at the appropriate time. All current family ties will be broken, even those to you. She will be an orphan of unknown parentage to prevent any possible repercussions of your current actions coming back on her. Do you need time to think on this offer?"

Amber couldn't believe how much like his father Rian looked and sounded. A moment of worry reared before she brushed it away. He was different to his father. Maybe there were some similarities, but that was to be expected. He'd been raised by Ronan.

"I accept," Daray said.

"Then who hired you to kill me?"

Daray looked towards Amber. "I didn't believe the offer that was sent out. I decided to find out if it was true. I haven't seen weight in gold offered in decades. I finally received a personal offer. I had a spy cam hidden on me in case they went back on their offer. I can give you the location of where I hid it."

"Who was it?" Rian's words had an edge to them.

"Paili, the head of Coyle Clan."

"You had better have flawless proof.

"Who is Paili?" Amber turned to Rian.

"Kiani's closest ally. She knows you are somehow involved with Ronan, but does not know the details."

"Kiani? Kade's mum?"

Rian nodded.

Amber turned her back on Daray, certain her face showed the shock she felt. Was it only Paili involved? Had Kade's family decided he shouldn't have a mage? That since they weren't willing to share how mages were made, then no one should have one? Amber desperately wanted to sit down. And possibly even throw up.

"Will you be fine?" Rian moved so he could look at her.

Amber nodded.

Rian examined her a moment longer before he turned back to Daray. "I need the location of your daughter and the proof. Ronan does not need to know about the girl and we should retain the original proof. You need not worry Ronan has recorded this session, the material the walls are made from interferes with electronics. But I guess you have noticed the benefits are worth that inconvenience. No one can send their thoughts into or out of this room. Or enter it from the Void. No one can hide in the Void listening to us, nor can anyone kept in this room be found by a tracker."

Daray gave Rian the information he requested and Rian ushered Amber from the room to where only Kade and Brann waited in the hallway. As soon as he saw her, Kade wrapped his arms around her.

"Where's Crystal and Flinn?" Amber asked.

"Ronan sent them home," Kade said.

Rian closed the door before he spoke. "Can you stay here until I return? I need to gather some evidence."

Kade's arms tightened around Amber. "Don't take too long. I want to get her home."

For once Amber didn't protest about someone making plans for her. With the chaos inside her head there was no way she could think clearly let alone make decisions.

"Who is it?" Brann asked.

"Paili. Kiani's closest ally." Rian's words brought silence.

"Are you certain?" Kade finally asked.

"I soon will be."

Silence filled the hallway again, broken only by the sound of Rian's footsteps. Amber pulled back from Kade. "Would your mother be a part of this?"

Kade shook his head without hesitation. "No. But Paili and Ronan are old enemies. Although none of us thought Paili felt that strongly about him to risk current ties. We were obviously wrong."

Amber turned when she heard a slight sound behind her. Ronan strode towards them. She was glad Kade kept his arms around her so she could lean back against him. She wasn't certain her legs could support all her weight yet.

"So who is it?" Ronan looked directly at Amber.

"Paili."

"That bitter old bitch? I thought she'd be over it by now."

"Over what?" Amber asked.

"Nothing. It's history. Are you certain? He wasn't just trying to save his life, was he?"

"Rian has gone to collect the proof," Amber said.

"Good. I'll see it's verified as soon as he brings it back." Ronan smiled at Amber. "And you doubted my plan would work."

"Guess I should know better by now." Returning his smile was too much effort, but she did allow herself a yawn. "I hope Rian hurries. I want to crawl into bed and sleep for a week."

"Does this mean you don't want to hunt down wyverns after all?"

At this comment Amber was able to dredge up a smile as she turned slightly so she could look at Kade. "Dream on." He wasn't going to keep her safe in his castle while he went out hunting. She wasn't the type to sit at home cowering in the shadows, waiting. He'd just have to get used to it.

Chapter Nine

Amber stared at the map spread out on the table in front of her, trying to suppress yet another yawn. She nibbled on the piece of toast she held and tried to focus on what Flinn said. Instead, her mind roamed and she glanced around the table to where Shannon sat beside Jasper, her warriors behind her, just like Flinn's were. Crystal sat beside Flinn and Kade was on her right while Maira and Brann were seated at her left. Rian stood behind her as usual. In the corner of the room sat a man taking notes in the folder he held.

Testing had already begun and she hoped the man hadn't noticed her inattention and was marking her down because of it. She tried to recall his name, but failed. It was something ordinary. At least she thought it was.

"Amber, Flinn wants to know if you and Kade are fine to take the northern entrance," Rian prompted her.

"I don't see a problem with that." Amber took a large bite from her piece of toast rather than smile like she wanted to do. It was a pity Rian couldn't walk in the Void. He would have been able to help her out in class. Maybe she could hire a Gold Warrior to do that for her. Suddenly everyone around her started to rise and Amber hurriedly rose to her feet.

"Do you need me to give you a quick explanation of the plan?" Rian asked.

She grinned at Rian. *"Was it that obvious?"*

"No." He returned her grin fleetingly. *"There are four exits. Only three Gold Warriors. The smallest exit, which is the eastern one, will be attacked by Maira, Orin, and Shannon's youngest warrior, Rhobert. Flinn's team have the west and Shannon's the south. You, Kade and Brann will take the northern entrance. Each team leader will keep communication open with their own group so everyone can hear the moment any attack plans are changed. And you were reminded to aim for the wings. They are not human and never have been. Think of them as rabid dogs."*

"And what will the scribe be doing?"

"Scribe?"

"The one sitting in the corner making a million notes about us."

"Along with his staff, he will watch you from the Void, making more notes. And the testing will not be over until you have all returned to the castle and taken care of the injured."

Amber stepped outside, popping the last piece of toast in her mouth. She really hoped that later she wasn't going to regret having something to eat, but she'd been starving. In the castle courtyard, three dragon saddles waited. Amber stood beside Rian as Kade, Shannon and Flinn were saddled.

"I never asked you what you did with Doneele last night." She glanced towards Rian.

"I left her and her granny at a motel. I'll find somewhere more permanent for them after this test. Do you need help mounting?" Rian nodded to where Kade waited for her.

Amber shook her head and then was nearly bowled over by Crystal who threw her arms around her.

"Good luck. I'll see you after we win."

Amber grinned as Crystal ran back to Flinn and hurriedly strapped herself into the saddle. She did the same. "Okay. Rabid dogs. I can do this."

"You better be able to," Kade warned her.

"I can." She held on as Kade launched himself into

the air, Brann and Rian on either side of him. As they drew closer to the wyvern nest, Rian dropped back so the 'scribe' could clearly see he wasn't interfering in the test.

Amber felt a moment of fear when the first wyvern flew out of the nest towards her. She couldn't resist reaching out with her mind to check that it was like a rabid dog. A shudder went through her as she made contact with its mind. Nothing sane there. Rabid dog was too kind a description. She momentarily froze, then all the hours of practice kicked in and she flung balls of fire at its wings. The screech it made as it plummeted to the ground brought more wyverns pouring from the nest. Amber's mouth fell open at the sight of them. They were meant to take out all of these?

She frantically threw fireballs as Kade dived in amongst them, slashing and retreating. Brann did the same and Amber had to keep an eye on where he was so she didn't accidentally hit him by mistake. At times, the day seemed full of shadows as the wyverns blocked the sunlight from them. With the way Kade flew, Amber was glad to be strapped in.

"Down."

She flattened herself against Kade, at his command, and felt the air rush by her as they slid through a crowd of wyverns. As soon as they were past, Kade wheeled and headed back to them. Amber sat up and launched two fireballs before she had to press herself against Kade again. This was going to take them all day. Or did they have the bulk of the creatures? Surely each team weren't fighting this amount of wyverns.

Amber soon learned the quickest way to deal with them was to throw fireballs at their wings. It was the same area Kade and Brann aimed for when they slashed at the wyverns. It was the wyverns and dragons' biggest weakness. From the heights they flew at, survival was impossible once the wings were disabled.

"Amber, are you hurt?" Kade asked.

"Her upper left arm. It's little more than a scratch. She should be able to heal it herself," Rian said.

Amber looked at her arm in surprise and noticed blood dripped onto Kade. A ten centimetre long gash ran along her arm. Pain burst through her as soon as she noticed it. She pressed a hand against the wound and focused on healing. She hated to think what Rian considered a gash if this was a scratch. It took her a few seconds to find the small amount of dragon blood running through her veins. It was only this that enabled her to heal.

"I think I've taken a bit more than a scratch." Brann angled down sharply, one wing barely working. Two wyverns took off after him.

Amber couldn't throw fireballs at the wyverns without risking Brann and was relieved when Kade flew towards him. Her relief was short lived when a cluster of wyverns came at them.

"I can't get to you, Brann." Kade took a quick turn to the left, trying to avoid the wyverns.

Amber clung tightly as she saw a wyvern grab hold of Brann and try to rip into his unharmed wing. Brann twisted in midair, trying to dislodge the creature.

"I can't get it off me," Brann called.

"Rian, help him," Kade ordered.

"If I help, you will fail," Rian warned.

Kade didn't hesitate with his answer. *"His life is worth more than the test."*

Amber took a deep breath. *"Hold off, Rian."* She unsnapped the harness and turned into a goshawk. Her smaller size made it easier to fly through the gaps between the wyverns. A second wyvern latched onto Brann and he started to rapidly lose altitude.

She reached Brann, claws outstretched as she tore at the second wyvern's wings. It left Brann to attack her. Amber darted out of the way of its barbed, serpent like tail and went for the wings again. She screeched in victory as the wyvern plummeted away and she turned back to Brann who struggled with the other wyvern. She harried it, going for the wings. It refused to let go. She aimed for the red eyes, barely being missed by sharp fangs as the wyvern's mouth snapped closed.

"You better deal with him fast, Amber. At this rate I'll have streamers instead of wings," Brann warned.

"This bastard is already flying streamers. If he'd just let go he'd be eating dirt," Amber said.

"He's not going to let go easy. I think his claws are–" Brann's thoughts became a roar of pain.

Amber launched herself at the wyvern, her wings wrapping around it as best she could. She tried not to think about what she was about to attempt as she became human.

"Amber! Do not do it. Whatever you are planning do not do it," Rian ordered.

Her human arms could barely hold the wyvern as it twisted and turned, trying to bite at both her and Brann. She felt fire pool in her hands and she forced it at the wyvern. Suddenly they plummeted towards the ground and she opened her arms wide, trying to focus on becoming a goshawk. She closed her eyes as she saw Rian hurtle towards her, claws outstretched to grab her. The change came and she opened her eyes to fly out of Rian's grasp at the last second. She headed back to Brann, who struggled to stay aloft.

"If you pull a stunt like that again I'll lock you in the dungeon." Kade wheeled in close. Several wyverns trailed him.

"Oh shut up. I managed it didn't I?" She landed on Brann's back. *"Hold steady and try to coast."* The moment he was, she became human. Her hands held on tight and her legs pressed against his sides as she tried to keep herself from falling off. She focused on healing Brann and watched in amazement as the tatters in his wings became whole. She laughed, letting go to become a goshawk as she dropped away from him. She flew towards Kade, ignoring Rian who followed as close as a shadow.

She wanted to shout with the rush of adrenaline that coursed through her veins from her stunt. Instead, she had to make do with the harsh cry of a goshawk. She landed on Kade's back. *"Steady."* The moment he was, she became human and strapped herself in again. She couldn't stop the grin that formed. "Yes! Let's kick some more butt!"

"I'm going to kill you later."

Amber could almost hear the growl in Kade's

thoughts. She ignored it to laugh and launch another fireball into the wyverns they flew towards.

Brann came up on their left. *"Don't worry Amber, I won't let him."*

After that, the battle seemed to go quicker, the wyverns thinning. At a glance below to the rolling green hillsides, Amber's feeling of victory became a rush of nausea when she saw the carnage they'd caused. She quickly pushed that image from her mind and focused on the one of Brann being attacked by wyverns.

"Flinn's team are waiting to enter the nest," Kade said.

"Damn. I wanted to be finished first," Amber said.

"I bet we have the higher body count," Brann said.

Amber shuddered. *"Great."*

Brann ignored the obvious sarcasm. *"I know, isn't it?"*

Amber couldn't help smiling as she threw another fireball. She looked around for the next wyvern and was surprised to see the sky was clear. "We did it."

"Not quite. We have to enter the nest and make sure there are none inside. Shannon only has a couple more wyverns to deal with and then we're all ready to go in." Kade landed and Amber slid off him, her legs nearly buckling.

"I'm going to ache tonight." Amber kneaded her thigh muscles.

Brann landed beside her and became human, quickly followed by Rian.

"Don't start relaxing yet. We might have a lot to get through still." Brann removed the saddle from Kade so he could become human.

"Time to head inside." Kade led the way, Rian the last to enter, on Amber's heels. They left the saddle outside.

Amber looked around. The large rough tunnel had plenty of space for a dragon to fly through. With the way her legs ached she half wished Kade had stayed in dragon form so she could have ridden. She soon found out why they walked.

"Over here." Brann pointed to some disturbed earth and quickly knelt to dig in it. He unearthed four eggs, which he and Kade smashed.

Along the tunnel, they managed to find another seven clutches of eggs. The sound of fighting filled the tunnel and Kade held a hand up to Amber. "Follow well behind and look out for more eggs."

Kade and Brann rushed ahead, becoming dragons as they did. Amber followed more slowly, Rian a couple of metres behind her. She carefully searched the tunnel, finding only one more lot of buried eggs.

Her attempt to put her fist through the egg, like Kade and Brann had done, failed.

"Show offs," she muttered under her breath as she threw the egg against the opposite wall. Her eyes shied away from the exposed contents and the other two eggs soon followed the first.

When Amber reached the central chamber, the fight was over and everyone searched for more eggs. Her eyes roamed around and relief poured through her as she saw everyone was there. They all had a few cuts and bruises, but they were alive and without major injuries. One by one, Amber checked them over and healed them. The last one she healed was Kade, who'd kept sending her to deal with everyone else first.

Kade pulled Amber back to him when she started to move away, one of his hands curving along her cheek. "You're looking pale. You haven't overdone it, have you?"

"I'm fine." Amber ignored the slight tremor exhaustion caused in her body.

Kade smiled. "Sure you are."

Amber returned his smile. "Can we go yet?"

Kade shook his head. "We have one more thing to find."

"What?"

"The best part."

A shout went up across the chamber and Kade linked his fingers with Amber's as he hurried her over to the group that formed around one of Shannon's warriors. Kade clapped him on the back as the warrior stepped away.

"Is that what I think it is?" Amber stared at the tumble of colour mixed with the dark soil.

"A wyvern hoard. They like shiny toys too." Maira grinned as she reached out to pick up an uncut diamond and hold it at her throat. "What do you think?" She posed theatrically.

"Bag it up." Flinn threw a hessian bag at her before he moved away from the group.

Crystal grabbed at Amber's free hand. "Oh my god, oh my god, oh my god."

Amber giggled. "Not as good as a castle though, is it?"

"Oh my god!"

Amber laughed, tugging her hand from Crystal's so she could drape her arm around her shoulders. "Think you might be able to say other words eventually?"

"Ohhhh."

"Catch," Maira called to Crystal as she threw a cut ruby towards her.

Flinn reached out and caught it before it hit Crystal, a glare sent to Maira.

Crystal took the ruby from Flinn to examine it closer. "It's real?"

"It's not made of glass if that's what you're wondering." Flinn turned to Kade. "Are you going to join Shannon and me to check for stragglers?"

Kade looked down at Amber. "I won't be long."

She nodded and leaned a little more heavily against Crystal, who was just about bouncing with excitement. Kade stared at her a moment longer like he was about to say something. Instead, he shared a look with Rian before he strode after Flinn and Shannon.

The three of them were back by the time the last of the gold and jewels were dropped into the hessian bag. Amber was surprised to see it was nearly half full. Crystal continued to hold the ruby Maira had thrown to her. She reluctantly walked towards the bag and started to put it in with the rest of the hoard.

"I don't mind if she wants to keep it." Shannon grinned. "I'm sure she's a dragon at heart and we all know how we are with the first hoard captured."

There were chuckles and smiles from the other dragons. Kade shrugged. "I don't care."

Flinn was the only one who didn't smile. "Given free and clear? Nothing owing?"

"No strings," Shannon said.

"Free and clear," Kade agreed.

Flinn nodded before he turned to Orin. "You're on first patrol."

Crystal clutched the ruby to herself. "It's mine?"

Amber grinned. "It looks that way."

Crystal danced across the chamber to Amber and wrapped an arm around her waist. "I seriously don't know how I'll explain this to Mum if she ever finds it, but I really don't care." Crystal spun around, taking Amber with her as she tilted her head back to stare at the cavern ceiling far above them.

Kade gestured towards Maira to follow Orin and Shannon's first warrior, she'd sent on patrol, then rescued Amber when she stumbled. "Time to go home."

As soon as they were outside, Kade waved Brann away from the saddle. He turned to look at Amber.

Recognising his expression, her hands went to her hips and her chin lifted. "Don't start."

Kade grinned. "I'm never letting you watch another action movie again. What did you think you were doing?"

Amber reluctantly smiled. "James Bond at your service."

Kade grew serious and reached out to brush Amber's hair away from her face. "Passing the test is not as important as your life. Or Brann's for that matter."

Amber shrugged.

"I'm serious, Amber."

"I got caught up in the moment. I don't like to lose."

"Keep this up and you won't see your seventeenth birthday."

"It's not that far away."

"Amber–"

"No. I'm tired." She held out her blood stained hands. "I also need a bath and I'm starving. Can you keep your complaints till later?"

Kade pulled her close, wrapping his arms around her. "Just take better care of yourself in future," he murmured against her hair.

"I do. I'm still alive, aren't I?"

Kade pulled slightly away to smile down at her. "Yeah. I guess you are." He swiftly kissed her and then waved Brann over with the saddle, turning into a dragon.

As soon as Brann had saddled Kade he helped

Amber clamber on. She leaned against Kade, giving into the exhaustion that tugged at her body, needing to be woken when they landed in the castle courtyard. Sliding to the ground, Rian caught her when her legs gave out. It seemed like seconds before Kade stood beside her as a human.

She leaned against him when he draped an arm around her shoulders. "I forgot to ask before. Did we win?"

Kade guided Amber inside. "They have to argue all their findings. It'll take a few days for them to decide."

"Where did Maira and the other two warriors go?" Amber stumbled on the stairs.

"Our warriors will take turns patrolling the area for the next forty-eight hours to make sure every last wyvern was dealt with. Occasionally stragglers return to the nest." Kade waited by his bed as Rian pulled the linen back.

"I need," Amber yawned, "a wash."

"It can wait."

"Hungry too." Her head hit the pillow and she didn't hear Kade's reply.

Chapter Ten

Amber woke with the sun, trying not to groan and wake Kade who slept beside her in dragon form. Every muscle in her body ached. Even her stomach. It was so empty she almost felt sick. Beside her, Kade became human as he slowly woke.

"Sorry." Amber rested her palm against his cheek, surprised to see her hands and arms were clean. She guessed she'd been more tired than she'd thought.

Kade turned his head so his lips grazed her palm. "Feel any better?"

"Worse. I need to soak for a week."

"Your bath will be ready in a couple of minutes."

Amber looked towards the door where Rian rose from a mattress on the floor. "Tell me you didn't sleep there last night."

Rian moved away from the door as it opened and

two women entered, taking away the mattress and bedding. "Your bath is ready."

"Rian? Did you sleep there last night?"

"You told me I was to say I did not sleep there last night." Rian strode across the room and pulled out a change of clothes for Amber.

Amber staggered out of the bed, grabbing the clothes Rian held out to her. "We will talk about this. You're not lying across my door. How comfortable is that for a place to sleep?" When Rian continued to remain quiet and expressionless under her glare she growled and spun on her heel, slamming both the bedroom door and bathroom one behind her. "Damn warriors," she muttered, knowing they could hear her.

Her mood improved dramatically when she slid into the bath and saw the plate of bacon and eggs set on a small table beside the tub. By the time she emerged from the bathroom, she felt almost human. It had helped that she'd figured out how to use her healing ability to take the stiffness from her muscles.

Back in Kade's room, Crystal sat on the bed waiting for her, the ruby lying in the middle of her crossed legs. "I was beginning to think you might have drowned."

"Glad to see you worried enough to check on me."

Crystal grinned. "Did you know we get a share in that hoard once it's valued and shared out evenly?"

Amber looked at Kade who nodded. She turned back to Crystal. "What will I do with part of a hoard?"

Crystal continued as if she hadn't heard. "And you can choose to have the value in gold, dollars or pick out some of the jewels."

Amber waved a hand in front of Crystal's face. "Are you still in there or have I lost you to that ruby?"

"Seriously. This is like a dream. Castles. Dragons. Pretty rocks." She held the ruby up. "Please don't pinch me because if I'm sleeping I'd rather not wake up."

Amber laughed, dropping onto the bed beside Crystal. She spared a glance for Kade and Rian and wondered what they were silently plotting. Deciding she'd deal with them later, she turned back to Crystal. "No dream. See." She pinched Crystal.

"Hey!" Crystal squealed, slapping at Amber's hand.

Kade approached the bed. "How about we go for a long walk? Unless you two had something else planned?"

"Why?" Amber looked between Kade and Rian and her eyes narrowed as she tried to figure out what was behind the offer.

"Because there's a lovely little creek I played in when I was a kid. I thought you might like to see it."

"That sounds cool." Crystal grinned. "If I can bring my new toy."

Rian rummaged around in the wardrobe then strode to the bed to drop a black drawstring bag in Crystal's lap. He turned to Kade. "Do you need me to collect anything?"

"A blanket and something for morning tea," Kade said.

Crystal popped the ruby in the bag. "Make that heaps of food. I'm starved."

It seemed like everyone wanted to go. Amber sighed. So much for having a lazy day. "I don't suppose we can get to the creek by car."

"We don't have cars. Can you ride a horse?"

"I love horses." Crystal hopped off the bed. "I'll run and tell Flinn where I'm going."

"Try not to invite him," Kade called after her.

"I can't ride," Amber said.

"You can sit behind me then."

Amber leaned back, her arms spreading out to the side as her head hit the mattress. "Only if I can be completely unenergetic."

Kade leaned over her, his hands resting on the bed,

one on either side of her. He slowly smiled. "I think that can be arranged."

Amber wrapped her arms around his waist, pulling him closer. "And I bet I could make you forget about picnics."

"Tempting."

Amber's eyes closed as their lips met and she could have throttled Crystal when she burst back into the room minutes later. Kade grinned down at her and then leaned back so he could offer her a hand up. Amber reluctantly took it, letting him pull her to her feet.

Kade's lips brushed her ear, his words quieter than a whisper. "You can mess with my memory later."

Amber couldn't resist a smile as he moved back, his gaze meeting hers. She nodded before she walked towards Crystal who waited impatiently.

"I can't leave you two alone for a minute without you finding the nearest bed. Or not even bothering with one." Crystal shook her head in mock disapproval.

"What did Flinn say?" Kade asked.

"Stop carrying that bloody rock around."

"About you joining us for a picnic," Kade prompted.

"That was it. I said I was going on a picnic with you and he just growled at me and said that."

Amber shook her head. Flinn was hard to understand sometimes. Well, maybe most of the time. They stepped out into the courtyard as Maira landed, a strange dragon with her. The dragon became a tall gangly man with black hair and a narrow, pointed face. He stepped forward, holding out an envelope to Kade.

Maira continued to stand where she'd landed. "I intercepted the messenger on my way in from my patrol, but he wouldn't let me deliver the letters. Said he needed to hand them over in person."

"You were out all night?" Amber asked.

Maira shook her head. Her gaze remained on Kade as he opened the letter. "We swapped over every three hours." She took a step forward. "How long does it take to read a letter?"

The messenger withdrew another two envelopes. "I also need to see Shannon and Flinn."

Kade gestured towards a man who entered the courtyard.

"If you will follow me, sir." The man held the door open and waited for the messenger to precede him.

"You're deliberately doing this, aren't you?" Maira tried to read the letter over Kade's shoulder but he closed it with a smile. The smile became a grin and he handed the letter to Maira. She squealed when she read it. "Our share of the hoard is a hundred thousand? Sweet!"

"How many shares are there?" Amber asked.

"Three. One for each Gold Dragon," Kade said.

"Do I get to pick out a pretty rock too?" Maira's gaze slid towards Crystal and then back to Kade, her smile pure mischief.

Kade took the letter from her and tucked it back in the envelope. He turned to Amber. "Do you want a souvenir from your first hoard?"

"I don't know. Maybe something little that I could wear on a necklace." Amber shrugged. "I don't know."

Rian chose that moment to lead two saddled horses with bulging saddlebags into the courtyard. He handed the reins of one horse to Kade and led the other to Crystal. She reached up to pat the horse.

"You know, just because I love horses, it doesn't mean I can ride them." Crystal continued to stroke the horse.

"I can." Rian swung up on the horse and held out a hand to Crystal. He helped her swing up behind him.

Kade also mounted, waiting for Amber to join him.

When she continued to stare up at him, he grinned. "You can walk if you want."

Amber sighed, reaching for his hand. She tried to smother the shriek that escaped and clung to Kade once she was seated. Her arms tightened around him as they started to move off. "This doesn't feel safe."

Kade laughed. "This from the girl who rides dragons with no parachute."

"Yeah, I know. But a horse just doesn't feel as steady. Besides, it doesn't understand me."

"How do you know? Have you tried talking to her?"

"Idiot," Amber muttered.

"Hold on." Kade urged the horse forward and they broke into a slow canter. Soon they were galloping across the rolling countryside, following a stream to where it forked off into a shady glade, becoming a little noisier as it tumbled over rocks.

Kade noticed Amber's smile when he helped her down. "Did you like it after all?"

"I like going fast. Slow just made me feel like I was going to slide right off."

Hearing her, Crystal came to stand beside Amber, her arm going around her waist. "How am I ever going to manage to return home after this holiday?

It's going to kill me. I've actually been thinking of quitting school early."

"Crystal! No! What about uni?"

"Oh, I'm not going."

"What are you going to do instead?" Amber dropped down onto the blanket Rian spread in front of them.

Crystal joined her, tucking her legs under herself. "Help Flinn." She grinned. "I've already warned him that if he doesn't treat me right that I bet there's more than a thousand other Gold Dragons who'd love my help."

"Probably way more than a thousand," Amber said.

"And I know you'd come looking for me if I seemed to drop out of existence."

"Of course I would." Amber glanced towards Kade and Rian who leaned against trees not far from them.

"We all would," Kade said.

"See. I'll be fine. But Flinn keeps harping on about me finishing year twelve since he has to. I tried to point out that not everyone does finish it, but he wouldn't listen."

"Well, whatever happens, I'll look out for you." Amber grinned. "You and your pretty rock."

Crystal grinned back. "I know, isn't it just awesome?"

Amber couldn't help laughing. "Can you imagine what your parents will say if they find it?"

"I'll tell them Flinn gave it to me." Her eyes danced with suppressed laughter. "And you can bet they won't be thinking saintly thoughts."

Amber's reply was interrupted by the sound of dragon wings. She turned to look up into the sky. A large blue and silver dragon, flanked by two other dragons, flew down. A look towards Kade and Rian showed that Ronan was expected.

Her first thought was to rise to her feet, but then decided it was better to remain relaxed. "Ronan, so nice of you to join our picnic. Although your son is a bit slack at serving." She sent a pointed looked towards Rian who brought one of the saddlebags over and started to unpack food and drinks. It would have been nice if they'd warned her Ronan was joining them. She was definitely going to have to say something about that to Kade later.

"It was your choice to keep him. If you get sick of him you can always send him back to me to deal with." Ronan stretched out on the edge of the picnic blanket, picking up an apple.

"He's a bit of a diamond in the rough." Amber shrugged slightly. "Oh well, I guess they do say diamonds are forever."

Ronan smiled. "Nice turn of phrase. But I wouldn't start getting too cocky. I don't think you're up to playing with the grown ups yet."

"What choice do I have?"

"A good point." Ronan took a bite from the apple.

"Other than looking for a feed, was there a reason you decided to join us today?" Amber tried to keep her words light, but curiosity was eating away at her.

Ronan turned to Crystal. "How many people can you see, including yourself?"

Crystal looked around. "Seven."

Ronan nodded before his gaze returned to Amber. "The proof is authentic."

"What's wrong with you people? Paili is meant to be Kiani's ally. Someone really needs to teach all of you what that means." Amber wanted to pace. Instead, she managed to stay on the blanket.

"Don't try and change our society. It won't work. You'll just end up disillusioned and then dead." Ronan tossed the apple core into the trees. He looked over to Kade. "Kiani needs to be informed. Quietly. And we need to make our alliance a little more public."

Kade nodded. "I'll invite my parents and some of my family to dine with us tomorrow night. We should know by then how our test went. That'll make a good excuse for the meal. Celebration or commiseration, either will do. Did you wish to join us or wait until Amber's party?"

Ronan tapped his finger on his chin. "I'll wait. I think that'll make a better impression. Surely you can keep her safe for six more days."

"That might be best. We don't want to risk Paili wondering what we might have learned by making too many changes too quickly," Kade said.

Amber tried not to ask, but she couldn't resist. "What have you done with Daray?"

"He's still where you last saw him."

"What are you going to do with him?"

"You can't have him."

She mightn't have asked, but she'd considered it. "I didn't ask for him."

"Amber, he's your enemy." Ronan's voice was filled with exaggerated patience.

"I know that." Maybe. "What are you going to do with him?"

Ronan rose to his feet. "I'll see you at your party."

"Ronan-"

"It's not up for discussion." He smiled. "Will you save a dance for an old man?"

"Can you dance?"

"A waltz." Ronan sprang into the air as he turned

into a dragon and was soon flanked by his warriors as he flew away.

Amber's mouth dropped open. "I can't waltz. Don't tell me that's the only dance you do at your parties."

Kade grinned. "No, we do the minuet too."

"I don't even know what the hell that is."

"Please tell me you're joking," Crystal said. "I don't know what it is either."

"Lucky there's plenty of time for dance lessons then." Kade joined them on the blanket, helping himself to a slice of cake as he ignored both expressions of shock.

Chapter Eleven

Amber watched as Kiani greeted Kade and congratulated him on passing yet another test. She handed him an envelope that he pocketed.

Amber glanced towards Maira who stood near her. *"What was that?"*

"A Gold Dragon's clan gives them fifty thousand each time they pass a test."

"Kade has one hundred and fifty thousand dollars from that one test?" Amber hoped the shock didn't show on her face.

"Nah. He'll give half of that fifty to Flinn since he doesn't have a clan. Everyone must be paid."

Amber started to shake her head, but stopped in time. *"What I really want to know is when he's going to give her the proof about Paili."*

"He would have already done that."

"*When?*"

"*When Kiani gave him the cheque.*"

"*I didn't see.*"

"*No one is meant to see, but it's the most logical time.*"

"*You dragons just like to make things complicated.*"

Maira smiled. "*We love complications. Not to mention intrigue, dramas and destruction.*"

Amber turned towards Maira, startled. "Destruction?"

"*Ask your warrior what his tat means.*"

Amber glanced towards Rian who stood a couple of paces behind her. "*What does your tattoo mean?*"

"*Creation, preservation, destruction.*"

"*That makes no sense.*"

"*They're all part of each other.*"

"*Great, now we're going to have a Yoda moment. I'm still not understanding here.*"

Kiani stopped in front of her. "Amber. It is lovely to see you again."

Amber forced herself to smile pleasantly and not growl in annoyance at the interruption. She couldn't think of a single word to say.

"How are you enjoying staying on our lands?"

She shrugged. "It's very green."

"Yes, I guess that's something you'd notice after living in your dry country," Kiani said.

"What the hell am I meant to say to her?" Amber appealed to Maira.

Maira smiled at Kiani. "It looks like everyone is starting to make their way to the dining room. Shall we?"

Kiani's gaze was drawn around the room. "Yes, of course." She led the way to the dining room.

Kade waited by the door for Amber and guided her to where she was to sit. The table was crowded with not only some of Kade's immediate family, but also some of their important allies. Amber was annoyed to see one of those people was Paili.

"Stop looking at Paili," Rian warned.

"She shouldn't be here." Amber stared at the plate of food that was placed in front of her.

"We can keep an eye on what she is doing while she is here," Rian said.

"I didn't realise it was going to be such a large dinner party." Amber glanced towards Kade as he started to eat his food. She picked up her cutlery and moved her food around, trying to figure out what it was. It appeared to be some type of stir fry drowned in a dark sauce. It suddenly occurred to her to ask, *"Is this what my birthday party is going to be like?"*

"Eat your dinner, Amber. People will wonder what the problem is if you do not at least try it," Rian said.

Amber took a small mouthful and finding it bearable had a little more. She looked across the table when she heard Crystal's laughter. She watched Crystal chat to the young man beside her, asking a million questions and totally at ease with her surroundings. Amber couldn't understand how Crystal could forget all their problems and just enjoy herself. She wanted to do something, not sit around and wait for someone else to make a move. She wanted to drag Kiani from the table and point at Paili and demand to know what Kiani was going to do. And if she planned to do nothing, she wanted to deal with it. Amber barely managed to stop herself from looking in Paili's direction again.

She could now picture the woman without even looking. Paili was only a couple of inches off six foot, black hair piled on her head and eyes nearly as dark. Jewels decorated her throat, wrists and ears ensuring everyone could see her clan was wealthy. What had surprised Amber the most was that Paili, like the rest of the dragons at the dinner party, wore well known designer labels from her world. She was glad she'd given in to Maira's choice of dress for her to wear this evening, but as always, she wore figure hugging dragon-leather shorts and top underneath her dress. There was no way she wanted to end up naked if she turned into an animal and then became human again.

"What time is it?" Amber asked Rian.

"The night is still young. Try and talk to someone. It is meant to be a social event," Rian said.

Amber couldn't resist a look in Paili's direction. *"Sitting down to eat with your enemies is considered a social event? Do you think knocking Paili flat would end the night sooner?"*

"You are not much of a pacifist, are you?" Rian asked.

"I said I wanted peace, not that I was incapable of standing up for myself." Amber bit back a sigh and made an attempt at eating some more of her dinner. How long could they draw this process out?

Amber soon found out they could draw the process out a very long time. It was after midnight when she finally managed to escape to Kade's room. She discarded her dress in a puddle on the floor and dropped onto the bed to stare at the ceiling. "I never want to endure another one of those meals. Please tell me I don't have to."

Kade closed the door behind him and looked down at her. "It isn't often I need to attend them."

"Then please go without me next time. I'm amazed I didn't fall asleep in my dinner."

Kade laughed. "I'm glad you didn't. The first thought everyone would have had would be poison. It would have caused a panic."

"You're kidding, right?"

Kade shook his head. "Not at all."

Amber groaned. "I'm never going to figure your world out." She started to say something when a woman entered the room and set up a solid looking fold out bed near the door, but she was too tired to get into an argument with Rian about where he was going to sleep. At least it was better than a mattress on the floor.

* * *

Amber was still thinking the same thing five nights later as Maira and Crystal helped her get ready for her party. It was the first time she'd used her bedroom. "What do you mean nothing has been done about Paili yet? And why does she have to be at my party?"

"Because these things take time and we don't want her to be suspicious. She'll already be wary when she sees Ronan arrive. We need to keep everything else as normal as possible," Maira said.

"Tell me again how many people are going to be here?"

"Thousands," Crystal interrupted. "I just can't wait to go down there. A ballroom! You're having your birthday in an actual ballroom. I really, really want to come back here in the September school holidays for my birthday. You should see how they've decorated the place. I can't wait to show you."

Amber groaned. "Great. Tons of people to watch me trip over my feet when I try and do those stupid old time dances."

Kade entered the room in time to hear Amber's complaint. He laughed. "You aren't that bad. Besides, it's only for the first part of the night. It's expected."

Amber turned to face him. "Your world has too many expectations." She fingered the topaz that hung at her neck. A souvenir from her first hoard, the gold chain a gift from Kade for her birthday. She planned to tell her family it was from all of them. "Do we really have to go down to the ballroom?" She slid her hands up the front of Kade's suit jacket.

"You look beautiful." Kade's lips met hers.

For several moments Amber forgot about the crowd waiting to help her celebrate her birthday. When she pulled away it was to find Maira and

Crystal had already left. Rian, as usual, was nearby. "Where did they go?"

"They will be in the ballroom. It is time for you to make an entrance." Rian held the bedroom door open.

Amber eyed the doorway as if it led to a pit of snakes. "When you said birthday party, I didn't think it was going to be anything like this. Most kids I know celebrate their seventeenth with some smuggled alcohol and a stereo turned up loud enough to annoy the neighbours."

"I want my world to see you're important. This is how we do things." Kade grinned. "If you want your noisy, drunken party we can have it Saturday at my house."

"But then it'd be Brann's party since that's the day he turns seventeen."

"I'm sure he'll share it. Now quit stalling. You're more valuable than any of those dragons down there waiting for you. You're the only Dragon Mage in all the worlds who can heal."

Amber sighed. "Fine. But if I make an idiot of myself I'm going to blame you forever."

"You won't. Now come on." Kade slipped an arm around her waist and guided her out of the room.

"I won't what? Make an idiot of myself or blame you forever."

"Neither."

As they drew closer to the noise of the ballroom, Amber's steps slowed until she barely moved at all. Kade stopped and turned to face her.

"We could be watched by any number of Golds right this minute. Are you sure you want them to see you act this afraid?"

Amber tilted her head back to glare at him, but he was right. Which she hated even more. Pushing Kade out of the way, she strode towards the ballroom. Kade fell into step beside her. Pausing, she waited for the doorman to open the door to the ballroom for her and then continued to stride forward.

The ballroom was a sea of faces, the centre of the room dotted with couples dancing to the orchestra that played in the far corner. Amber froze. A waiter walked past and Rian took a glass, handing it to her. Even after a couple of mouthfuls, she couldn't have said what she drank.

People came over to her, their words a blur. She smiled and hoped that would be response enough. Her glass was taken from her hand and the next thing she knew, she was waltzing with Kade in the middle of the room. Slowly her brain started to function again and she began to recognise faces in the crowd. Her grip on Kade loosened and when she looked up at him, he smiled.

"Look at that. You're still alive."

"But you mightn't be by the end of the night."

Kade laughed, spinning her around fast. *"And after all the trouble I went to for you."*

"Trouble I could have done without."

"I'm not hiding you away like I'm ashamed of you."

Amber wondered if there was another meaning behind his words. *"You don't think I do that, do you?"*

Kade shook his head, his smile still in place. *"No. I understand. It might annoy me sometimes, but I also know it annoys you too. So I can live with it."*

"Mind if I interrupt?" Jasper tapped Kade on the shoulder.

Amber grinned at her brother as he waltzed her around the room. "This is nothing like my last birthday party."

Jasper laughed. "I've barely seen you these holidays."

"I guess we've both been busy."

"I feel like I should be saying thank you a million times. This has been the most amazing holiday."

"And that wouldn't happen to have anything to do with me catching you kissing some girl the other day?"

Jasper laughed again. *"Not at all."*

After that, Amber lost track of how many dance partners she had. She finally had to beg off to rest her feet and grab a drink. As she took a mouthful of fruit juice, she was surprised to find she was smiling and actually having a good time. Well, other than the few times she'd caught a glimpse of Paili.

Across the room from her she saw Ronan talk to an older couple. He looked over as if he felt her gaze on him. He nodded in her direction and she smiled.

"You haven't danced with me yet, Ronan. And after you told me to save you one."

"What are you playing at now?"

"Nothing. Just using you. Weren't you the one who said something about unity?"

Ronan turned back to the couple he'd been talking to and seconds later he strode across the room. Amber handed her glass to a passing waiter and watched as Ronan drew close.

He held out his hand to her. "Happy birthday, Amber."

She took his hand. "And I didn't even have to phone you so you could say it."

Ronan laughed as he whirled her onto the dance floor. *"And how are you finding the evening since they dragged you down here."*

Amber grinned up at him. *"You see. That's why I said it's pointless for me to lie to you. I'm watched by too many of your people."*

"It's not only my people who watch you."

"I'm beginning to feel a great deal of sympathy for the celebrities in my world who have to deal with the paparazzi."

"Is that what you want, Amber? To be famous? Come and see me when you're eighteen. We can forget about the offer I made for you to marry my heir. I'll marry you myself. You would be the most famous woman in our lands."

"I'm flattered Ronan, but I'll have to decline. When you wanted to end it, I'm sure I'd have worse than a broken heart. You'd probably rip it out."

Ronan laughed. *"I might be tempted, but as you pointed out, I don't break my word. Between us, we could rule this world."*

"I want enough power not to be a target. I think ruling the world would put me on the top of every single person's hit list."

"Do you doubt I could protect you?"

"I'm not one for cages."

Ronan smiled. *"Maybe we do have some similarities after all."*

Amber was curious about the fleeting expression in Ronan's eyes, but before she could ask him, the world exploded around them. Ronan shielded her as rock and glass rained down, the nearby wall shattering to be replaced by thousands of dragons pouring into the ballroom.

The air was filled with screams, yells and roars. People shouted at each other. Some ran, others flew from the ballroom and some attacked the warriors that continued to pour in. Amber was torn from Ronan's arms by the confusion and twin balls of flames appeared in her hands as she raised them. Before she had the chance to throw the fire at those attacking, a dragon grabbed her like a rag doll.

Her last vision of the ballroom was of Ronan, surrounded by dragons and none of them his own. Amber struggled to escape, but the claws tightened around her. She couldn't breathe. The world grew hazy as she gasped for breath. Haziness was replaced by blackness.

Chapter Twelve

Cold seeped into Amber's bones as she became aware of her surroundings. Her eyes opened and she stared at a stone ceiling. Struggling to sit up, she realised she was attached to a wall by a short chain. Checking her surroundings had her guessing she was in a dungeon and she wasn't the only occupant. Across the room, Ronan was chained to a wall by each limb. He wore only dragon-leather pants and his body was scored by claw marks. The gashes caused a steady drip of blood to create a puddle at his feet. She guessed it wasn't the grey metal that deadened dragon powers since Ronan was still human.

Amber staggered to her feet terrified he was dead. She forgot for a moment he would be a dragon if that was true. "Ronan!"

His head was tilted back, his eyes closed. Slowly he faced her. A trickle of blood ran down the side of his head from a wound on his forehead. "We should have moved against her sooner. None of us expected her to do anything at such a public celebration."

"You're alive."

"For now."

She ignored that uncomfortable thought. "Are you certain it was Paili?" Amber tugged on the chain but she couldn't get any closer.

"No, but who else wanted to finish you off?"

"Whoever it is, wants to finish you off more than me."

"There you go then. It's definitely Paili." Ronan coughed and blood flecked his mouth. He leaned his head back against the wall and closed his eyes.

"No! You're not going to die. Do you hear me, Ronan?" She tried to reach out with her mind to call for help beyond the walls. It was impossible. She guessed the walls were made of the same material Ronan's prison was made from.

"Sheathe your claws, little kitten. There's not much either of us can do." Ronan didn't even bother to open his eyes.

"That's it? You're giving up?"

Ronan finally opened his eyes to look at her. "I know I've been a bastard most of my life, but surely even I don't deserve to be harassed while I'm hung up to die."

"You aren't going to die and leave me in here alone."

"Be realistic, Amber. I'm working on making a swimming pool here, with my own blood."

She stared at the single chain holding her to the wall. She'd already examined the cuff and seen it was too tight to change into a panther. Not knowing where it'd be on her as a bird, she wasn't game to try that option. With her luck, it'd be her neck. At best, she could break a wing. Her gaze was drawn to Ronan and she worried that he was right. She wasn't about to tell him that though. "Stop being so melodramatic. It's only deep enough for mice."

Ronan laughed and then started to cough again.

"Oh shut up, Ronan. You're making yourself worse." Refusing to give into fear, she stared at her chain. Holding a hand against it, she formed a fireball. She swore when that didn't work.

"You're wasting your time, Amber. While you were passed out I was busy discovering that there's no escape from here."

She ignored Ronan and turned her attention to where the chain was embedded in the wall. The metal in the wall was different. Hopefully different enough for the heat to do its job. She watched the loop as she increased the heat of the fireball she held against it. Nothing changed. She used more energy, making it even hotter. Sweat started to pour down her body. Then the metal buckled under the onslaught and Amber pulled on the chain. She nearly yelled in victory, but kept quiet since she didn't know if anyone would be able to hear her. She ran to Ronan's side.

"Ronan." She placed her hands against his chest and tried to ignore the blood that instantly coated them.

"Go. Don't waste time. I'm further gone than Rian was."

"Stop talking crap. You're too old to carry on like that." She started to heal some of the wounds.

"Amber. Stop! I'm barely holding this form as it is. If I become dragon, the chains will tear me apart."

She stopped immediately. She didn't know if she had the energy to set him free and heal him. What choice did she have? How long would they be left alone? She had to do something. He couldn't expect her to stand there and watch him slowly die. She didn't have it in her.

Amber strode to the only exit. The lock seemed simple enough. She held her hands against it and heated it until it melted. Now it would be impossible for them to use a key. But as for getting out, she didn't know how they were going to accomplish that. After she'd freed Ronan she would worry about it.

She worked on the chains that held Ronan's legs first. She felt a wave of weakness rush over her as the second chain twisted free from the wall, but she couldn't stop. She needed to break at least one more chain, just in case he couldn't hold his human form. Her legs barely carried her the few paces. Leaning against the cold rock, she tried to gather her strength.

"Why are you doing this?"

Amber met Ronan's gaze. "Because it's the right thing to do. Why aren't you demanding that I help you escape?"

"Because I gave you my word not to harm you. So get out of here before I decide my life is worth more than my word."

"No."

"Why?"

"I already told you. Helping you escape is the right thing to do."

"What? No pledges of eternal friendship?" His smile was more a grimace.

Amber laughed softly. "No. We are friends, but that isn't why I'm doing this."

"We aren't friends Amber. We made a deal so I could use you to get my lands back."

"Yeah, but I kinda grew to like you along the way even if I don't always like what you do." Which had surprised her too. She'd never expected to like him even a little bit, but she guessed she couldn't blame a wild animal for following its instincts. "And don't forget, you're my adopted uncle. I've got a weakness for family and friends. Haven't you pointed that out to me before?"

"This weakness is going to get you killed."

Amber grinned, trying not to focus on her surroundings. She didn't want to give into the fear that threatened to bring her to her knees. "Kade tried to tell me I wouldn't make it to my seventeenth birthday with my refusal to listen to his so called good sense. I guess he was wrong. I even had the party to prove it."

"Shut up you bloody fool and get out of here."

"How sweet. I didn't realise you cared for me so much."

"I don't. You're going to make me break a promise if you don't go. I've never broken a promise in my entire life."

"Sure." Amber gathered her energy together and forced a ball of fire against the chain that held Ronan's left arm to the wall. She sagged to the ground as it came free, barely able to hold onto consciousness.

"Amber!"

"Stop bitching," Amber muttered. She closed her eyes and breathed shallowly as she tried not to throw up. The cold stone against her back helped. Her head pounded, or was that sound outside her head?

"What did you do to the door, Amber?"

"Huh?" She looked up at Ronan and tried to make sense of his words.

"The door." Ronan gestured towards it.

"Do you think they brought food?" She was starved.

"Amber!"

"Stop shouting." She clutched her head.

"Then focus."

She tried to get to her feet, but it didn't work. She crawled closer to Ronan. "I am."

"What did you do to the door?"

"Melted the lock."

"It won't hold them forever."

"Okay." Amber leaned against the wall, closing her eyes again. She screeched when Ronan grabbed a fistful of her hair and started to pull her up. "Let go." She struggled to her feet and met his gaze, surprised to see there were gold flecks in the blue. She frowned. "You're not Gold."

Ronan swore. "Amber, either get rid of this last chain or run. I can't protect you when I'm chained to the wall."

Her eyes closed again. "That's okay. I'll protect us." A flame flickered to life in her hand and went out instantly.

"Amber, are you listening to me?"

"I never listen. Ask Kade." She sagged against Ronan who hissed in pain. Opening her eyes, she stared at his chest. "Sorry." She pressed a hand against him and tried to heal him some more. The blood slowed to a trickle, but the wounds didn't disappear. "Sorry." The word was slurred as she slid to the floor, barely noticing the puddle of blood she landed in. "Sorry."

"Never mind. You gave it a good shot." Ronan sat beside her, pulling her close with his only free arm. "Sleep."

"Night." The cold of the wall kept her from falling completely asleep so Amber tried to snuggle into Ronan more. There was barely a difference in temperature. She fought against exhaustion, knowing this couldn't be right. She peered up at him, his arm stretched tight from the chain that attached him to the wall, the other around her. "You're cold."

"Shh." He pressed her head back against him. "Rest. When they finally break through that door, you turn into a hawk and get out of here. I'll wake you when it's time."

"I can't leave you behind." She struggled to sit up. "And what if the chain on my wrist snaps my wing?"

"Risk it. What have you got to lose? Just get my lands back. You can have them. Or your Gold for all I care. I'd even rather my youngest had them than the treacherous bastards who currently hold them."

"I need food. That'd give me more energy." Amber peered around, but no meal arrived in front of her.

"There's plenty of blood lying around."

"Oh please, don't make me throw up."

"Turn panther, she won't mind."

"I will mind." Amber pushed away from Ronan, staggering to her feet. She eyed the last chain in the wall. There was one other fact she hadn't shared with Ronan even though she knew it would have made the most sense to him. She wasn't about to tell him since it was the only reason he'd believe and her reasons were far more complicated than having just one. He was her only ally she could trust and without him to help, she didn't know how she'd fare in a world that believed in survival of the fittest.

"Don't even think about it, Amber. Save your energy to fly out of here."

She ignored Ronan's words and forced as much heat into the chain as possible. The link broke free as everything went black.

Chapter Thirteen

Amber came to and found herself pressed against a blue dragon. She rubbed her eyes, groaning as she noticed the dried blood on her hands. She wondered if she was seeing things. There were little flecks of gold in the silver veins of the dragon's wings. She reached out to touch a fleck. It didn't come off.

Ronan grumbled deep in his chest and Amber looked towards his head. He didn't look good. His head rested on the ground and his eyes were dim. But even then she could still see flecks of gold in them. She placed her hands on him and knew he needed more healing. He tried to pull away but he was too weak. Amber healed him some more and fought against the wave of nausea that shook her body. When it passed, she snuggled up to Ronan again and drifted back to sleep.

She was woken what felt like seconds later by a

banging at the door. She grinned as the door continued to hold. She wondered what they were using to try and break it down. Maybe they needed explosives. She guessed they could get hold of them since that was probably what had been used to break into the castle. Amber frowned. Had the rest escaped? Especially Crystal, Jasper, Kade, Rian, Maira and Brann. She had to get out of here. Had to find them. No, they had to get out of here. Her and Ronan.

Amber forced herself to sit up again and heal Ronan some more. Beneath her hands he flowed back into human form, grabbing her wrists to pull her away from him. Chains rattled.

"Stop it. There's no point in killing yourself to heal me."

Amber smiled. "I never thought I'd hear a comment like that from you."

"Shut up," Ronan growled.

"What happened to everyone else?"

Ronan rose to his feet. "I don't know."

"We need to get out of here."

He stared down at her, disbelief evident. "Haven't I been saying that all night?"

Amber tried to get to her feet, but the room spun around so she lay down instead. "Right after I have a rest." She closed her eyes.

Ronan dragged her roughly to her feet. "Get up. We can't stay here forever."

Amber tried to pull away, but she had no energy. "Another five minutes. Please."

"That might work on your mother, but not me. Now heat these bars up so I can get you through them." Ronan pushed her up towards a barred window.

"I can't. I don't have enough energy."

"Then I'll slit a wrist and feed you blood. People have been known to survive on it for ages."

Amber knew Ronan wasn't joking. She forced herself to heat the bars until they buckled and bent. She huddled against the wall when Ronan lowered her to the floor so he could finish off the job.

"Get up."

Amber looked at the arm Ronan held down to her, the rest of his body on the other side of the window. It seemed a long way up. She closed her eyes. "In a minute."

"Now!"

Amber muttered under her breath as she struggled to her feet. "Why did I think it was a good idea to save you?" She held out her hand and Ronan grabbed her by the wrist, hauling her up the wall. "Hey!" The rough wall scraped against her body, removing skin in several places.

"Quit whining. You're starting to annoy me." He hoisted her over his shoulder and slid through the Void. Ronan dumped her against the wall of a dark alley, the sound of their chains echoing around them. "Stay here."

"Can I sleep now?"

"No."

Amber sighed, trying to keep her eyes open. It was impossible. Then she was being roughly lifted off the ground.

"Be careful," Ronan ordered.

Amber relaxed again.

"One minute we're kidnapping her, the next we've got to treat her like glass," Hound muttered.

Amber's eyes flew open. "Hound?"

"What?"

"Just shut up and get her in the car. I need to get out of here," Ronan ordered.

Hound dumped Amber in the back seat of a four-wheel-drive and Ronan climbed in beside her. The sound of the engine lulled Amber back to sleep so the next time she woke it was to find someone putting a drip in her arm.

"Hold still." The man was going bald, had an excess

of weight and faded brown eyes behind his wire-rimmed glasses. "There we go. You'll be as good as new in no time."

Amber eyed the drip. "I'd rather chocolate."

Ronan chuckled from an armchair beside her bed. "Behave and I'll have them bring you some."

Amber struggled to sit up. "Crystal-"

"Rest. I've sent Hound and Tory to see what happened."

Amber relaxed, yawning. "So tired."

"That's the problem with exhaustion. You sometimes hallucinate." Ronan stood, leaning over her as the man left the room. The door closed softly behind him.

Amber met Ronan's pale blue eyes. There were no flecks of gold in them now. She smiled. "I'm not an idiot. But I also know when to shut up."

"You could have fooled me. I could have sworn I had to tell you several times."

"I'm not your enemy," Amber said quietly.

"I'm not your friend."

She grinned. "I know. You don't have friends. That's why you're my uncle. Family's more important than friends anyway."

"You can't just adopt people."

"Yeah, you can. Crystal, she's family too." Amber yawned. "I can't believe how tired I am."

"Go to sleep. But we're still not friends."

"That's okay, Uncle Ronan."

* * *

Amber was woken by a whispered argument. She struggled to sit up, smiling when she saw Rian.

Rian turned on Ronan. "Now you have woken her." He strode to Amber's side and helped her sit up, rearranging her pillows so she could lean back into them. "Do you need anything?"

Amber shook her head and looked from Ronan to Rian. "What were you arguing about?"

"Your warrior wanted to know how I could let you get in such bad shape and not have a scratch on myself. He thinks you wore yourself out healing me."

"You owe her a life. I saw the state you were in when they took you from the ballroom," Rian argued.

Amber put a hand on his arm. "We saved each other. I healed him so he could get us out of there." Her gaze met Ronan's. "We're even. No debt on either side."

Ronan's eyes narrowed. *"Are you sure?"*

It had to be that way. Ronan was too proud to accept any other option and she needed things to stay the same. An ally she could trust, not one resenting her. Amber nodded. "Even."

Ronan turned to Rian. "You heard her, boy. We saved each other."

The door burst open and Crystal flung herself at the bed. "Amber!" She swiped at tears with the back of her hand. "I thought they'd killed you."

Jasper and Kade followed Crystal into the room. Jasper went to his sister's side, while Kade turned to Ronan.

"Who was it?"

"I never saw her, but we were held at one of Paili's smaller castles."

"She has to die," Kade stated.

Ronan nodded. He turned to the doorway where Tory stood. "You can leave if you wish."

Tory shook his head. "I chose sides long ago."

Amber frowned. "Sides?"

"Paili is my mother."

Amber stared at Tory. "That's why she hates Ronan."

Tory nodded. "She didn't want me. I wasn't Gold. But she didn't want Ronan to have me either."

"Why?" Crystal now sat beside Amber on the bed.

"Because she's very possessive of what she sees as hers," Tory said.

Rian glanced towards Ronan. "It is a common dragon trait."

"If it's mine, no one is welcome to it unless I give it to them. Even if I have no use for it," Ronan said.

"What about Rian and Hound? Is she their mother too?" Amber asked.

"No." Ronan looked towards Amber who yawned. "Everyone out. You're tiring Amber."

"It's okay," she yawned again. "I'm not that tired."

"We'll be back later." Crystal slid off the bed.

Jasper patted her on the shoulder. "Rest."

Ignoring Amber's protests, everyone started to leave. Her gaze met Kade's. *"You're not going to leave too, are you?"*

He smiled, moving closer so he could sit on the edge of her bed. "Never." He took her hand.

Relieved, Amber's eyes drifted shut. "Good."

Chapter Fourteen

When Amber woke the next time, she found Rian standing at her door and Kade dozing in the armchair by her bed. Even though his eyes were closed, he was still human so he couldn't be properly asleep. She stretched, finally feeling like she'd live. Kade sat up at her movement.

"How do you feel?"

"Good." She glanced at the drip. "Good enough to get this thing out."

Rian moved to her side and lightly pinched her skin. He nodded and started to remove the drip.

"Why'd you pinch me?" Amber asked.

"You were extremely dehydrated when the doctor hooked you up earlier." Rian held a cotton wool ball against her arm as he removed the drip and then taped the cotton wool down with a band-aid. "A light meal will be here in a minute."

"Thank you." She turned to Kade. "Did anyone else get hurt at my party?"

"No one was killed. They took off as soon as they had you and Ronan. They escaped through the Void, all headed in different directions." Kade rose to stand by the bed, taking her hand. "She will pay for this."

"Don't get mad, get even?"

Kade smiled, but it was not a friendly smile. "Precisely."

"Kade, I don't know-"

"If we let her get away with this everyone will think they can do the same. Survival of the fittest."

"Stupid rule," Amber muttered.

"But it is a rule and not one that any dragon who wishes to live would ignore."

"If you seriously want peace, then give me your funeral plan," Rian said.

"I don't want a war."

Kade shook his head. "Do you understand anything we've told you?"

"Yes. But we don't need a war. We just need to get rid of Paili," Amber said.

"Kill her," Kade corrected.

Amber winced, wanting to protest.

Ronan entered the room. "What do you suggest other than war, Amber?"

"I don't know. But there has to be something. Crystal can see through the Void, you can enter it. There's got to be something we can do." Amber frowned as she tried to figure out a plan.

"I'm sure we can come up with something in the next couple of days," Ronan said.

"Amber needs to go home to her family tomorrow," Rian said.

"It's Saturday?" Amber looked from Rian to Kade who both nodded. "What about my ordinary party? And where is Brann? I haven't wished him a happy birthday."

Kade grinned. "You just escaped death and you want to party?"

"Can you think of a better reason to celebrate?" Amber demanded.

Kade took hold of her hand. "No."

Amber met Kade's gaze and wished they didn't have an audience. She ignored that thought and turned to Ronan. "So what do we do about Paili?"

"Give me a week or so to come up with a plan."

Amber nodded. She hesitated. He was her ally, even if it was reluctantly. "As long as they're not in the Void, I can tell you how many people are in a residence from outside the building."

Ronan continued to meet her gaze, finally

nodding. "That will help." He started to leave the room, then turned back. "Try not to get yourself killed or captured. I really hate having to replan once I settle on one."

Amber grinned. He'd never admit it, but maybe he was becoming her friend. "I wouldn't dream of inconveniencing you." The moment the door was closed, she turned to Kade. "Now, about my party."

"It's very short notice."

"And?"

"Open party or limited invite?"

Amber tugged Kade closer. "Open party. Did you forget something earlier?"

His lips were a breath away from hers. "I can't imagine what it might be." His lips brushed hers before he kissed her.

Amber wrapped her arms around Kade. When he pulled back she smiled. "Much better." She pushed him away slightly. "But now I'm starved. Go and find out what's taking my breakfast so long."

"I will get it. It is waiting in the hall for you. They did not want to interrupt when Ronan was in here." Rian strode across the room and opened the door. He returned seconds later with a tray.

* * *

Amber sat quietly beside Kade, Rian on the other side of her. Maira drove while Brann sat passenger. Amber held onto Kade's hand. Every kilometre closer to home made her grip tighten. The party last night had been a great finale to a pretty good holiday. Well, apart from being kidnapped. Flinn had convinced Jessica to have it at her home so Kade's place wasn't trashed. But Amber thought that was only because he and Crystal had stayed at Kade's place last night and he hadn't wanted to have to kick everyone out once he'd had enough of the party. Considering how popular he was, socialising was not something he liked to do. Amber could sympathise with him. Ever since everyone had thought she and Kade were together, she'd gained a lot of friends she didn't need. Not a single one of them sincere.

Kade reached over with his other hand, loosening her grip. He grinned when she looked up at him. Amber looked away. She didn't want to talk to anyone. Or see anyone. In particular her grandmother. It wouldn't have been so bad if she'd had enough sleep. Even getting to bed not long after midnight hadn't helped. It was the dreams that had disturbed her sleep.

Each one had been the same. Trying to stay afloat in a large lake. No matter which direction she looked, she couldn't see the shore. And no matter how long she swam in any direction, it still didn't appear. Worst of all, the lake had been filled with blood. She didn't need to be a genius to figure out why she was having nightmares. She probably would've been more worried if she didn't have at least a few bad nights. A few more nights and she should be fine. She hoped.

Maira pulled up in front of Helen's house. Rian held the door open for Amber, who reluctantly slid out of the car, looking around. It all seemed far too ordinary. She crossed her arms, glad of the jacket she wore. It wasn't just the cold of the late afternoon that seeped into her. This would never be home. A shiver went through her. Was anywhere home?

Kade slipped an arm around her shoulders. "What do you want to do?"

Amber shook her head. How could she tell him when she didn't have a clue? She took a deep breath. For now, she had to go inside. She shrugged off Kade's arm. It was best they kept things platonic in front of her family for now.

Amber took her bags from Brann. "I want to do

this alone." Well, as alone as one could be with a Gold Dragon shadowing her from the Void.

"Rian will wait in your room for you. I'll return after dark," Kade said.

It was almost an anticlimax to find only her mother in the kitchen. "Hi, Mum."

Donna stared at Amber. "Are you all right?"

Amber forced a smile. "Yeah. Tired. We stayed up late last night. It was the last night after all."

Donna moved forward to give her a hug.

She returned it, feeling awkward.

Donna held her at arms length. "Are you sure you're fine?"

Amber nodded. She searched for a way to change the topic. "See what everyone gave me for my birthday?" She held up the topaz that hung at her neck. She'd been glad to find she still wore it after being kidnapped.

"That looks very expensive, Amber."

She shrugged. "Maybe that's why I only got the one present." She searched the house with her mind, only finding Rian in her room. The rest of the place was empty. She frowned. "Where's Grandma?"

"Visiting friends."

That was a surprise. She had no idea who'd want

to be friends with her grandmother. "I'm going up to my room." She lifted her bags a little. "To unpack."

"Did you take any photos?"

"Crystal has them. I'll get her to email you some of the best ones." After she'd checked to see there was nothing inappropriate in them. Like a dragon or two. Amber gestured towards the door that led out of the kitchen. "I'll unpack."

Donna nodded and Amber felt her mother's gaze on her as she hurried upstairs. Dropping her bags, she locked the bedroom door behind her and fell onto her bed to stare up at the ceiling. "I don't belong here," she muttered.

Rian lifted one of her bags and gestured towards the ensuite with his free hand. "There's a gift sitting on the vanity for you."

Amber sat up, looking through the open door to a small black drawstring bag. It seemed like a long way to walk when all she wanted to do was crawl under the blankets and forget about the past few days. Curiosity finally dragged her from her bed and she pulled the bag open to tip a rainbow of jewels across her vanity. Her shower being turned on made her look up in surprise.

Ronan pointed at the door. "Close it."

Amber looked towards Rian who methodically

unpacked her bags. He glanced up and gave her a small nod. Once the door was closed, Amber pushed the jewels to the side and perched on the edge of the vanity. She watched Ronan, too tired to care about games.

Ronan crossed the small room, grasping her chin to tilt her head up. Amber looked away from him, tugging out of his grip. She pushed at his chest until he took a step back.

"What do you want, Ronan?" She gestured towards the jewels. "And what's with them?"

"Are you already regretting you saved me?"

"No."

"Then what's wrong?"

"Haven't you heard? I was at a party last night. Sleeplessness tends to make me irritable."

"I thought you weren't going to bother lying to me."

Amber stared at him. Surely he couldn't know about her nightmares.

Ronan grinned suddenly. "I haven't learned to read blocked minds yet." The grin vanished. "You didn't sleep more than half an hour at a stretch last night. So let's try this again. What's wrong?"

"Bad dreams." Amber shrugged. "Nothing important."

"Don't you humans rave about the importance of talking about these things?" Ronan held up a hand when Amber started to speak. "And not to me. First an uncle and now you're going to try and turn me into an agony aunt?"

Amber smiled weakly. She picked up a dark blue jewel, holding it up to Ronan. "And these? I hope they weren't to cheer me up. I'm not so easily distracted."

Ronan shook his head. "Homework."

Amber frowned at the jewel in the palm of her hand. "That doesn't look like any homework I've ever done before."

"This is between you and me, Amber. No one else. Understand?"

Amber met Ronan's pale blue eyes, noting the hardness. "How can I? You haven't explained a single thing."

Ronan took the jewel from her and tossed it amongst the others. "You could have got out of that dungeon without my help. Why didn't you?"

"We saved each other. Are you still worried about the debt? There's none. We already sorted this out yesterday."

"As if I'd argue it in front of a witness. But we both

know better. I was dying and you risked yourself to save me. Why?"

Chapter Fifteen

Amber pushed off the vanity to pace the small confines. She finally turned to face Ronan who leaned against the door, his arms crossed over his chest. She could have given him a reason he understood, but it wasn't the main one. "Because I can't walk away from anyone."

"That's a liability."

"In your world."

"In any world." Ronan stepped forward, taking her by the shoulders. "Don't you understand? You could have been out of there in minutes. Flown home and been safe."

"That's if the chain didn't break my wing."

"That wasn't your only option. You still could have got out of there easily on your own."

"You would have been dead."

"And that's your problem, why?"

Amber shrugged, dislodging his hands. "I don't know." She turned away. "I know I should have left you. It made sense to get out of there. But I couldn't do it. You're the worst father, a complete bastard, but…" her words trailed off and she turned back to him. "I couldn't leave you to bleed to death."

"You keep trying to see me through your modern eyes."

"Then how should I see you?"

"I've made sure people think there are older dragons than me. But I am the oldest, Amber. Only you and I know that. I was born in the Dark Ages. I am what those times made me. A survivor."

"Dark Ages." The words were a whisper as Amber stared in disbelief.

"We didn't mark off the years so you'll have to forgive me if I can't give you an exact date. But let's say it was the year 500AD. I learned to fight against Vikings. Does that give you a clearer picture?"

Amber opened her mouth. No sound came out. She closed her mouth and tried again. "Vikings?" She sat heavily on the toilet lid, her mind wanting to shut down. Instead, it jumped tracks as it often did and she looked up at Ronan, a smile forming. "Do you think you can hide in the Void and help me with my next history test? You could pass the answers along to

Rian who I could station outside and he could tell the answers directly to me."

Ronan stared at her for a moment before he laughed. "You're a natural. Stop fighting against yourself and enjoy your power. You could have nations at your feet, Amber."

"Only if I let you stand beside me to enjoy the adulation I'm guessing."

"We would be unbeatable."

Amber shook her head. "No, Ronan. That really isn't me. I just want to live my life, not run everyone else's."

"You would make an amazing queen. You could rule forever."

"And why would I want to do that? What's the point in living forever?"

"Point? Why do you need a point? You humans and your imbecilic quest for the meaning of life."

"Then why have you struggled to stay alive all these centuries if there's no point or meaning?"

Ronan stared at her for a moment. "If there ever was a meaning it's been lost in the passing of centuries. Now," he shrugged as a smile formed. "The desire not to let someone else win after all this time is what drives me. Even the ones who are long dead. I won't let them win either."

"Is that enough?"

"Obviously. I'm still alive, aren't I?"

Amber laughed. "Yeah, I guess so. Although if I was better at following orders you might not be."

"Which brings us back to them." Ronan gestured towards the spill of jewels. "This is for you alone. I don't care how attached you are to your family, but if you can't promise to keep this secret between us, I won't give it to you. They aren't like you. They don't push themselves past the point of good sense."

"It's not deliberate."

"Do I have your word?"

"I don't know. What if it would help them too?"

"This is for you alone. Do I have your word or will we forget I ever visited today?"

Amber stared at the jewels that looked like there were twice as many from being reflected back at her from the mirror over the vanity. Keeping secrets from Crystal hadn't worked out very well last time. "I don't know, Ronan. I'm not good at keeping secrets from Crystal. She knows me too well."

"Then how about we make it essential you keep this secret. If she finds out our earlier deal is made void."

"Then no. I can't risk everyone like that."

"Even if what I have to tell you has the potential to not only save your life but others?"

"Then why not just tell me with no strings attached?" Amber glared at Ronan. It was at moments like this she couldn't believe she'd saved his life.

"You'll inherit my journals if I die. For now, the knowledge is mine to do with as I wish. And I wish to attach strings."

Amber was torn. Did he tell the truth? Could she ignore something that might save lives? She thought of Rian as he lay at her feet, surrounded by his own blood. Of Ronan's blood spilling onto the dungeon floor. No wonder she had nightmares about a lake of blood. She met Ronan's gaze. "This bargain has nothing to do with any earlier ones made. I'll keep it along with all your other secrets, Ronan."

"You only hold one secret. That of my birth year." Ronan's eyes were ice cold.

"I'm not colour blind, Ronan." She refused to be cowed. "There's a big difference between gold and bronze."

Ronan stood in front of her, taking hold of her chin. His voice dropped low. "It's safer to be colour blind."

"Just like it would've been safer to leave you there

to die?" Amber left her words hang, waiting for Ronan to answer.

Eventually he turned away from her, grabbing a handful of jewels with his right hand. He let them spill into his other hand. "Your life is the price for breaking your word." One jewel was in his right hand. A blood red teardrop. He held it out to Amber. "Deal?"

Her life. She smiled at the irony of it. Only Ronan would offer her something that could both save her life and cause her death. She wasn't about to tell anyone and risk their first deal too. She wouldn't have even considered accepting if she wasn't so worried about keeping everyone safe. She took the jewel, her fingers closing around it. "Deal."

Ronan held up another jewel, tossing it to her. Amber caught the diamond in midair. She looked at him with a question in her expression. He grinned. "You're going to learn to wear jewellery."

The questioning look became one of confusion. "And how will that save my life?"

"Mages once learned how to put their power into jewels so they could draw on it when they needed extra. Only the mage who had put it there could see the power in the jewellery. And only their power could be drawn back into them. There were a rare few who could use the power stored by others, but not many had that ability."

"How will that save lives?"

"If all your friends lay dying, who would you save? As it is, you have a limited amount of power. Would you choose Crystal? Kade? What about your brother? If you were surrounded by a sea of their blood, how would you be able to tell which one needed help the most?"

The imagery of a sea of blood was too close to her nightmares. She grasped the diamond tighter, her hand moulding to the facets. "How do I do it?"

"You practice." He took the ruby from her and tucked it into her jacket pocket. "Not with this one."

"Practice? That's it? No explanations? No magic spells?"

Ronan laughed. "I couldn't walk through the Void back when there were Dragon Mages. When it was decided no more should be made, their secrets died with them. I only have my observations."

"When did they stop making them?"

"Middle Ages." He gestured towards the jewels on her vanity. "Practice. When you learn I'll give you jewellery to wear."

"That's going to be difficult to explain to Mum."

"I'm sure you'll manage." Ronan turned, reaching for the door.

"Ronan?"

He faced her again, leaning against the closed door. "What?"

"What do you really look like?"

"You ask the oddest questions."

She stepped closer. "I know you change at least your eye colour. What do you look like?"

Ronan changed before her eyes. He was only a little taller than her, more muscular and younger, as if he and Rian were the same age. His pale blue eyes were flecked with gold and his hair was white blond. The lack of age made him look less dangerous. "Curiosity will probably be your downfall."

"Thank you."

Ronan nodded, changing back as he turned and opened her door. He didn't even acknowledge his son as he strode across the room, opening the French doors. He stepped into the Void as he walked out onto the balcony. Amber continued to stand there, her mind tangled with a million thoughts.

She looked at the diamond she still held. How was she meant to practice when her every moment was watched? Her gaze travelled across the room to where Rian stood by her door. Unable to bear any more scrutiny, she closed the bathroom door and turned off the shower.

Amber surveyed her bathroom. How much time could she spend in here without feeling like the walls were going to close in on her? It looked like she was about to learn.

Chapter Sixteen

Kade tapped softly on the bathroom door several hours later. "Amber? Are you okay? Can I come in?"

She pushed her hair away from her face, staring at the shards that littered her vanity and floor. This was impossible. She couldn't figure out what to do. Every time she tried, the jewels exploded.

"Amber?"

She wrenched the door open. "What!"

Kade glanced behind her. "What are you up to?"

"I thought it was time to take up a new hobby. What does it look like I'm doing?"

Kade glanced at Rian, which annoyed Amber even more. She pushed past him, striding to her bed. If they wanted to discuss her, let them. She was tired. Not to mention exhausted. Ronan had left her an impossible task. Forming a ball of fire in her hand, she felt the energy within. It was too much. The jewels were too fragile for so much power.

Amber pulled a thread out of the fire. The rest started to follow, rushing to join the thread. That was the problem. The force of the power shattered every single jewel it came in contact with. What could she do different?

Rian came to stand beside her, the black drawstring bag held up. "What would you like me to do with your confetti?"

A smile tugged at the corner of her mouth but she refused to let her anger go. "Find a bride to throw it over." She frowned. Maybe that was it. The jewels might be too small. But Ronan had said the power could be stored in jewellery. For all she knew, they wore necklaces the size of boat anchors back in the Dragon Mage era.

Pulling out her phone, she ignored Kade who joined her on the bed. She watched Rian put the bag of jewel shards away in her duchess before she flicked through her contact list and dialled Ronan's number.

"Don't tell me you've figured it out already."

"I need more. Try something around the size of a soccer ball."

Ronan laughed. "And where would you wear it? In your crown?"

"They're too small. They keep shattering."

"Then slow down."

"I'm trying. Just get me more, Ronan."

"Yes, Your Highness."

"And you can shove your crown where the sun don't shine." She hung up on his laughter.

Kade leaned over her. "Do you want to tell me what you and Ronan are planning?"

Amber shook her head. "I can't. He promised to kill me if I told anyone."

"Are you mad? He's dangerous. And I don't care if his Gold informs him that I think he is. Every sane dragon believes exactly the same. How many people, Ronan included, have to tell you he doesn't have friends?"

"Keep your voice down," Amber hissed. "Do you want my mum up here? It's my first day home. I don't want to get grounded already."

"It might keep you out of trouble."

Amber pushed him away so she could sit up to glare at him. "I doubt it."

Kade's glare became a grin and he chuckled. "You're probably right."

Amber dropped back onto her pillow so she didn't give into the temptation to return his grin. Her effort was in vain when he followed her. "Go away," she muttered.

"You don't really mean that. You're just tired and hungry. That always puts you in a bad mood." Kade moved closer, his body half over hers.

Amber could feel her anger start to evaporate. She tried to hang onto it. "Then leave me alone so I can sleep."

"Not even a kiss goodnight?" Kade's lips were close enough she could feel his heat.

Her anger finally faded and she reached up to pull him close. Seconds spun into minutes and Amber even forgot they had an audience, until the French doors were flung open. She nearly grinned at the sight of Hound, hands held out in a sign of surrender as her and Kade sprang apart to land on the floor, ready for battle, and Rian held a gun pointed at him.

Amber extinguished the balls of fire in her hands. "Where the hell did you get that from? Put it away, Rian." She waved towards the gun before she turned back to Hound. "What do you want?"

He withdrew two items from his jacket and held out a drawstring bag identical to the one Ronan had given her. In his other hand was an emerald the size of an emu's egg. "Errand boy."

Amber's mouth dropped open as she stared at the

emerald. It took her several seconds to regain the power of speech. "Didn't he have one the size of a soccer ball?"

Hound grinned. "His message for that comment is that you can have the soccer ball when you learn how to keep it intact."

Amber smiled as she imagined Crystal's expression at seeing a jewel the size of a soccer ball. They all turned at the knock on Amber's door. She searched the other side of the door and relaxed when she sensed it was her mother.

"What?"

"Dinner's ready. Didn't you hear me call up before?"

At a glance around the room, Amber guessed it had been when Hound had entered. "No. I'll be down in a minute." She motioned to Rian to take the jewels and lowered her voice. "Put them in the ceiling. Including the other ones. Mum'd freak if she found them."

Hound handed over the jewels. He held a sealed envelope out to Amber. When she didn't take it, he said, "Here," shoving it into her hands before he left.

'Read without prying eyes.' Amber smiled at the words scrawled across the front and retreated to her bathroom. She tore it open and grinned.

'Enemies are less costly. Burn this.'

It was so typical of Ronan. Very little that he did was straightforward. Everything had to be hidden. She held the letter and envelope over the sink and called fire to her hands. The paper darkened and flaked apart to fall in the sink. She washed it down before she headed downstairs for dinner, ignoring the curious looks of Kade and Rian as she shut her bedroom door on them.

Amber paused in the doorway to the kitchen. Her grandmother sat at the table, her back to Amber, her mother was at the sink rinsing off some dishes. Neither knew she was there yet.

"Inconsiderate. Never thinks of anyone but herself. Are we meant to eat a cold meal?" Helen's fingers drummed on the table.

Donna continued to silently rinse dishes. Amber wished she had that ability. It just wasn't her. Was it too late to run back upstairs and beg Kade to take her to his family's castle? She straightened her shoulders. No. That seemed too much like giving in. She mightn't fit here, but that didn't mean she was going to let her grandmother send her running. She wouldn't hide. That definitely wasn't her.

She strode into the room and dropped into her seat. "Did you miss me, Grandma? I was tempted to steal the silver and bring it back for you. I bet you would have loved it. But I kind of think the castle servants would've missed it."

"You stayed in a castle?" Donna joined them at the table. "You never said that. I thought you were staying at Kiani's home."

"That is her home." Amber picked up her cutlery.

"If you don't talk that boy into marrying you on your eighteenth birthday, you're an idiot." Helen pointed her fork at Amber.

"We're not even dating," Amber said.

"Then what are you waiting for?"

"Mum!" Donna glared at Helen. "Please. We talked about this. I thought we decided you were going to stop pressuring Amber."

"I never agreed to anything." Helen turned to Amber again. "Well, are you an idiot?"

"Probably. You'll have to blame Dad. He must have read me too many fairytales when I was a kid. You know, Prince Charming, dragons, love and happily ever after."

"The love and happily ever after come once Prince Charming slays the dragons," Helen said.

"Hmm, maybe I had different fairytales to yours." Amber took a mouthful of the well-cooked steak. She would have to remind her mother again that she only liked it medium these days.

"Dragons are always evil." Helen pointed her fork at Amber again. "Don't you forget it."

Donna slammed her cutlery down. "Do you pair have to argue about everything? Even fairytales?"

Amber said "Of course," at the same time as Helen said, "Yes."

"You couldn't get through one day." Donna rose to her feet. "And you're just as much to blame, Mum." She pushed away from the table. "You pair can clean up. I'm going to bed."

Helen ignored Donna, turning her attention to Amber again. "Where was this castle you stayed in?"

"Europe."

"That's a big area. How about being a little more specific."

Amber shrugged. "I gave up trying to pronounce the name. They all kept laughing at my attempts."

"What's on your necklace?"

Amber pulled the topaz out from the neck of her jacket. "They gave it to me for my birthday." And for kicking wyvern butt. She wondered what her grandmother would say to that information.

"Is it real?"

Amber grinned. "Yeah. They talked about a

matching set. Earrings, bracelet, you know. But I thought Mum'd have something to say about it."

"Next time forget about what Donna would say. You take the full set." Helen shook her fork at Amber. "Understand?"

"Yep." Amber finished her meal, rising to her feet.

"And do the dishes. You're younger than me."

She bit back the words that wanted to spill and put the plug in the sink. She could do this. It was only until the end of school. Then she was out of here. She didn't know where she was going, but she wasn't sticking around. She could last that long. Maybe.

A chair scraped across the floor. "Goodnight, Amber."

She glanced over her shoulder. "Night."

"And make sure you get more jewellery out of those kids. And start dating the boy. You've only got a year till you're eighteen."

Amber could only nod. Any words risked letting laughter escape. And she knew her grandmother was perfectly serious. She turned back to the washing up. At least now she'd have an excuse for accepting jewellery from Ronan. She could tell her mother that her grandmother had told her to take it. That was if she ever learned how to fill them with her power.

Looking at her hands in the water, she made fire

start to form. A flicker danced under the suds, competing with the water to stay lit. Amber stared at it and she slowly smiled. Maybe, just maybe, she'd finally figured it out. Rushing through the dishes, she ran upstairs. Before she could open her door, her mother came into the hallway.

"Why's your door locked, Amber?"

She reached out and turned the handle, swinging the door open. She watched as Kade and Rian disappeared out the French doors, glad her mother was at the end of the hallway. "It's not."

Donna strode towards Amber. "It was when I came up." She looked into the room.

"What were you doing going into my room anyway?"

"I was trying to see if you had any washing after being away."

A hand went to Amber's hip. "You don't wash this late at night. Why were you really going through my room?"

"It was locked so I didn't go through your room, did I?"

"You tried to. Is that what it's going to be like? No privacy?"

"I worry about you, Amber. You didn't seem

yourself when you came home. And you hear all sorts of stories about the designer drugs rich kids use."

Amber glared at Donna. "I don't do drugs and neither do my friends. I'm tired. Jet lag. Did you expect me to be bouncing around? I've got school tomorrow. How excited am I meant to feel about that prospect after a fortnight in a European castle?"

"See, maybe it isn't such a good idea for you to hang around these kids. You'll never have their life. It'll only make you dissatisfied with your own if you keep spending time with them."

"Who says I can't? Not everyone is born with money. Haven't you ever heard of self made millionaires?"

"Oh Amber, be realistic." Donna sighed.

"Well in that case I guess I'll just have to take Grandma's advice and marry Kade for his millions." Amber stepped into her room, slamming her door shut and locking it. She rested her head against the timber, ignoring her mother.

She felt Kade come up behind her, brushing his lips against her ear. "Was that a proposal?"

Amber turned to face him, her hands resting on his shoulders. "I don't know. I'm sure I can do much better than you."

"Who? Ronan?"

Amber smiled. She wasn't going to tell anyone about Ronan's offer. "I was thinking more along the lines of Prince Charming. Do you know him?"

"I think he was eaten by a dragon."

Her smile became a grin. "How terribly sad. I guess I'll hang around with you until I find a better offer."

"How gracious of you."

"I know." Amber couldn't hold back a yawn.

"Looks like that jet lag is catching up on you. Bedtime."

Amber was tempted to argue. She wanted to test her new theory on a jewel. Another yawn urged her to use caution for a change. She'd try again tomorrow. When she was rested.

Chapter Seventeen

Amber looked about as she floundered in a sea of blood. Around her floated the bodies of her friends and family as they moaned and begged her for help. She couldn't save them. She had no power left. She didn't even have the power to save herself. Again she sank beneath the blood red waves, trying desperately to struggle to the surface.

Striding across the waves came Paili. She wore a crown with a jewel as big as a soccer ball in the top of it. "Off with their heads." She waved a hand regally towards the bodies that crowded around Amber, begging her for help.

Heart racing, Amber woke, keeping her eyes closed as she tried to slow her breathing. This was the third dream tonight, each one worse than the last. So much for getting to bed so she could wake well rested. She ignored the temptation to check the time on the alarm clock beside her bed. The last thing she needed was for more reports about her sleeplessness to get back to Ronan.

"Amber?" Kade pulled her close. "I know you're awake."

"So?"

"What's wrong?"

"Nothing." She pulled away from him, striding to the bathroom with a glance towards the alarm clock. It was only two. She couldn't survive another night like last night. Closing the door, she turned on the light, glaring at the manhole. How was she meant to get the jewels down?

Biting back the words she wanted to mutter, she swung the bathroom door open. Rian stood there. He looked towards the manhole and then back to Amber. She nodded and he came in, hopped up on the vanity and stretched over to the manhole. He removed the drawstring bags and the large emerald. When he dropped lightly to the floor he handed the items to Amber and left the bathroom, quietly closing the door behind him.

Amber locked the door and ran water in the sink. She eyed the emerald but decided to leave it to last. Tipping the new jewels onto the vanity, she picked up the largest one. A sapphire. Holding it under the water, she took a deep breath. A flame flickered to life, barely warming the water. She fed a thread of it into the jewel and tried to control the rush of the rest of the flame when it wanted to follow. It was easier to control under water.

The jewel shimmered and then shattered. Amber swore, then glanced at the bathroom door. No one disturbed her. She took a deep breath and chose a different jewel. She held a diamond under the water, calling up another flame. This time she stopped the moment the jewel shimmered. She lifted the diamond out of the water and stared at it. She felt her power, like something live, trapped inside it. Excitement rushed through her and she wanted to shout. She had to make do with a grin.

Flinging the bathroom door open, she held the diamond out to Rian. "Tell me about this."

Rian took the diamond and examined the damp jewel. He met her gaze with a shrug. "A diamond. Flawless."

"Nothing else?"

"No."

"Are you sure?"

Kade crossed the room and took the diamond from Rian. "What's going on, Amber?"

"What are you holding?"

"A wet diamond."

Amber threw her arms around Kade and kissed him. She grabbed the diamond off him and closed herself in the bathroom again.

"Amber?" There was concern in Kade's voice.

"Quiet." She grabbed another jewel and held it under the water. This one shattered. Amber tried to tamp down her excitement. She couldn't control her power to the level it needed to be controlled when she was this excited. Several deep breaths and she was able to fill another jewel with power. Amber stared at the ruby she held. How did she get the power out of it? Closing her fingers around the jewel, she felt the power straining at the confines. She called it and felt a flare as it returned to her, seeming to be greater than when she'd put it inside the ruby. Was it only jewels?

Amber dropped the ruby onto the vanity and opened the bathroom door. She ignored Kade and Rian as she rummaged through the items scattered on her duchess. She gathered a pair of gold hoop earrings, glass slippers on a silver bracelet and a plastic bead necklace. Hurrying back to the bathroom with them, she soon found plastic didn't work, glass and silver were reasonable, but the power loved gold and rushed over the metal like flames on petrol soaked timber.

She took her necklace off and held it under the water. First she filled the topaz and then the gold. The chain was easier to fill than her earrings had been and Amber guessed it was due to the quality. When she was finished, she put it back on and slid to the floor, completely exhausted. Leaning against the timber door of her vanity, she couldn't keep the goofy grin off her face. She didn't even have to look in a mirror to know it was goofy. It felt like it.

"Amber?"

She turned to look at the door that separated her from Kade. She'd invite him in, but didn't have the energy to open the door. "Yeah?"

"Can I come in?"

All of the internal doors had external locks and could only be opened by a key from the other side. "If you can." It didn't surprise her much when a moment later the lock clicked and the door swung open, Rian stepping out of the way.

Kade sat beside her on the tiled floor. "Have you sorted it out?"

"Yep." The grin stayed in place.

"You still can't tell me?"

"I wish. I'm bursting with it. I want to tell everyone." She looked up as Rian handed her phone to her. Her grin widened. "Of course." She called Ronan.

"It better be good."

"I did it."

"Of course you did. So why did you need to ring me at," Ronan paused a moment, "nearly five in the morning."

Amber giggled. "Because you wouldn't let me tell anyone. I've got people all around me and I can't share it with any of them."

"I guess you want some jewellery now."

"Yes. And make sure the settings are gold. As pure as possible. Gold is definitely my medium."

Ronan chuckled. "I'll send Hound with a delivery later today."

Amber thought of the ruby teardrop Ronan had given her. "And I have a blood red ruby I want turned into an earring."

"Should I find a matching pair?"

"I doubt you'll find another one like it. I'm sure it's unique. A bit like friends. They're all irreplaceable."

"Get some sleep, Amber. You've obviously been awake too long. You're starting to sound like a greeting card. The kind that are only good for fire starters."

Amber giggled. "I don't need fire starters so I might just hang onto that greeting card."

"Goodnight, Amber."

"Good morning, Ronan." She laughed as he growled and hung up.

Kade wrapped his arm around her, drawing her close. He pushed the door closed. "Do you realise we're actually alone for the first time in ages?"

Amber looked up at him. A rush of heat went through her that had nothing to do with her powers. "What do you plan to do about it?"

Kade smiled as his head came closer. "I'm sure I can manage to think of something."

* * *

Amber heard her alarm and reached out to turn it off, only to bang her hand on the vanity. She struggled to wake up, trying to untangle herself from Kade's limbs.

His arms tightened around her. "Rian's got it. Sleep a little longer."

Amber lay back against him. "I can't believe we slept on my bathroom floor."

"Speak for yourself. There's no room in here to become a dragon."

Amber laughed softly.

"You're heartless."

She pressed her hand against her heart. "Nope. I've still got one. I can feel it beating."

"Prove it."

Amber squealed as she suddenly ended up lying on the tiles, Kade above her with his head pressed to her chest. Her arms wrapped around him and she held tight. It was moments like this she could forget everything that had happened recently. But it seemed like it didn't take much for it to come pouring back.

Kade pulled back slightly. "Are you okay?"

"I will be."

"What happened when you and Ronan were kidnapped?"

She still hadn't been able to tell anyone more than the basics. "I already told you. We were chained up in a dungeon."

Kade lightly kissed her. "Whatever happened, it was Paili's fault. Not yours."

"Nothing happened. I just don't want to talk about it. Now let me up. I can't be late my first day back at school."

Kade rose to his feet and helped Amber stand. She

chased him from the bathroom, took the clothes Rian held out for her and shut the door so she could take a shower. While she had breakfast, Rian tidied away the jewels and returning to her room she took the teardrop from her jacket, asking him to make sure Ronan got it.

When Maira pulled up out the front to give her a lift to school, Amber reluctantly left her room. Out of habit, she tried the two locked doors in the hallway and wished she knew how to pick locks. She stared at them thoughtfully and wondered if Rian would be able to unlock these doors too.

Hurrying down the stairs, she grabbed her lunch and called out goodbye to her mother and grandmother. Racing to the car, she grinned when she saw Rian and Kade in the backseat.

"Don't tell me you're going back to high school, Rian." Amber buckled her seat belt.

"No. The Gold will watch over you while you are there. I will go to Kade's place and sleep."

"You could sleep nights. There's always a Gold watching me."

Rian shook his head. "Assassins favour places with few witnesses."

Amber instantly regretted starting the conversation. That was the last thing she wanted to hear. She had enough trouble sleeping as it was. Looking over to Kade when he took hold of her hand, she smiled in answer to the query in his eyes. Maybe if she kept telling enough people she was fine, she'd start to believe it too.

Chapter Eighteen

By the end of the school week, Amber wanted to drop from exhaustion. And it wasn't due to the amount of jewellery she'd filled with her power. Not to mention the crystal on her duchess and even the mirror in her ensuite. She was surrounded with power she could tap into. But it hadn't stopped the nightmares.

All Amber wanted to do when she got home from school was collapse, but her mother waylaid her in the kitchen. Amber sighed, shifting the weight of her schoolbag. The six gold bracelets on her left arm jangled. Ronan had a craftsman make them for her and you could barely see the gap that was filled with the dragon-leather that they had been cast with. Now she knew what to look for, she realised her necklace had a similar safety link. On her other wrist a plaited dragon-leather band was filled with round polished jewels, each in a separate, decorative gold setting. The blood red ruby teardrop hung at her right ear.

"Sit down a minute, Amber."

Amber dropped her bag on the floor and sat on a chair at the table. She waited for her mother to talk. She wasn't about to spill any secrets just because an uncomfortable silence stretched between them.

"Is there anything you'd like to talk about, honey?"

"No."

"Is something bothering you?"

"No."

Donna sighed. "Amber, talk to me. I know something's wrong."

Amber stared at her mother. She had to say something. It looked like the interrogation would go on all afternoon and she had better things to do. "I'm not sleeping well."

"Why?"

"Nightmares."

"But why are you having nightmares, honey. What are they about?"

Why did her mother have to keep pressing for information? Especially since she couldn't tell her what she was dreaming about. The idea that popped into her head made her pause. She'd obviously been hanging around Ronan far too much, but it'd do the job.

"Amber?"

"I wake up in a strange place and can't find my way home. Then when I eventually get home, the house is empty. You, Dad and Jay are all missing."

"Oh."

The silence stretched out. "Can I go to my room now? I want to get my homework finished before Jay arrives for the weekend."

Donna nodded. Still silent.

Amber headed up the stairs and into her room. She was glad only Rian was there. At least he wouldn't say anything negative about what she'd said. She locked the door behind her.

"Was anything you told your mother true?"

Amber stared at Rian. Maybe she was wrong. "I've never had a dream like that in my life. Well, not that I can recall anyway."

"It will work. When you leave home at the end of year twelve, she will not try and force you to stay. Guilt will make her let you return to Brisbane."

"What makes you think I'll leave at the end of year twelve?"

Rian smiled momentarily. "My time is spent

anticipating your every need. I have even found a suitable house for you."

Amber stared at him. "Really?"

Rian nodded. "I have employed a woman to take care of it for you. She has a daughter, but the child is well behaved. She will be no bother." Rian stared at Amber. *"It is a good cover for Doneele and her granny."*

"I want to see it."

"Next time you are in the city."

Amber grinned. "Maybe you do know me after all." She couldn't wait to return to Brisbane.

Rian nodded. "There is a change of clothes on the bathroom vanity for you." He bent to pick up her schoolbag.

With a nod, she headed for the bathroom and had a quick shower. When she entered her bedroom again, her homework was laid out on her desk, ready for her to start. Afternoon tea was beside it. She took a bite from one of the biscuits laid neatly on the plate as she sat and started her homework. She was nearly finished when she sensed her brother pull up out the front. Shannon's warriors flew high above to guard him.

Pushing her schoolwork aside, she stretched, tracking his progress with her mind. He paused in the kitchen to greet their mother and then followed her to the sewing room where their grandmother was. Amber was tempted to go downstairs to see him, but she didn't want to risk another interrogation from her mother. Or get into an argument with her grandmother.

They'd already had one at breakfast. Finally Amber sensed Jasper come upstairs by himself. She rose to let him in. "You took your time."

Jasper entered the room and looked around. He stared at Amber and then crossed the room to pick up one of the crystal containers on her duchess. "What the hell have you done to the place?"

Amber closed and locked her door. "What do you mean?" She looked around. Everything seemed the same to her. The only difference was the glow of her power on numerous objects.

"Can't you see it? Feel it? You and this room are crawling with power."

Amber crossed the room in seconds, pulling the crystal from Jasper. She pushed him towards the seat at her desk. Panic flared and she tried to control it. "Sit down and don't say another word."

"But–"

"Are you trying to get me killed? Shut up." Amber took her phone from her pocket and rang Ronan. "Get over here right now."

"Don't order me around, little girl."

"I didn't say a word. Jay can see it. Now get over here before you're given the wrong information and think you have to kill me." She waved Rian back to the corner he'd been relaxing in.

"Why do you have to make everything a drama? I'll be there as soon as I'm ready."

"Then call your Gold and ask him for a word by word of everything that has happened since Jay entered my room. And there were no words spoken in our minds."

"Amber–"

She moved the phone from her mouth. "Sit down and shut up, Jay."

Ronan laughed. "Amber, relax. I'll soon know if you speak the truth. I'll bring some items for your brother to look at."

"You have other jewels that are…" her voice trailed off, not knowing how to word it without giving any information away.

"I'll see you later, Amber."

"Okay." She put her phone away when Ronan disconnected and stared at her brother.

"Can I move now? And speak?"

"It depends on what you might say."

Jasper looked around the room. His gaze landed on every item filled with power. "I guess there are some things it would be best not to discuss right now." He rose to his feet, lifting the pendant at her neck before he let it fall back against the front of her jacket.

"Yeah. You'll have to save your questions for Ronan. I can't answer them."

Jasper nodded. "Just answer me one question."

"If I can."

"Is this what keeps you up at night?"

Amber shot a glance at Rian who shook his head. That only left Kade who must have told Jasper. "No." It mightn't be what kept her awake, but it was what she did when she couldn't sleep.

"Next time you're online, google post traumatic stress syndrome."

"Don't you start."

"Have you looked in a mirror lately?"

"I'm fine."

"No, you're not. You look like you're living in a war zone. And Mum asked me to speak to you."

So maybe it hadn't been Kade. "She's already done that today."

"Yeah and it made her even more concerned. She thinks you're on drugs. I was about to suggest she get you tested and then I wondered if that would be advisable with the possible alterations becoming a mage might have caused."

"Nothing will show in a blood test," Rian said.

"How do you know? There are only three of us," Amber said.

"Ronan made the doctor run a lot of tests on you when the two of you escaped. He wanted to make sure there was no other reason, other than exhaustion, that you would not wake."

Amber stared at Rian a moment, then realised he wouldn't have allowed the tests if they weren't for her benefit. She nodded and turned back to Jasper. "So now what? I should go down there and tell her to test me for drugs if she's so worried?"

Jasper put out a hand to stop her when she started to march across the room. "Amber. Calm down. Just keep it in mind the next time Mum asks."

Amber shrugged his hand off her. "I'm sick of people telling me to calm down."

"Well, you are a little on edge lately."

"A little!" Amber glared at Jasper. "Paili is still out there." She waved towards the French doors. "And she has the money to pay for more than a thousand warriors to attack all at once."

Kade walked in the French doors. "She wouldn't do that where there are human witnesses. Even the warriors wouldn't. They could be killed for risking that type of exposure."

"What are you doing here so early?" Amber's gaze travelled from Kade to Rian. "Did you call him?"

Kade reached for her. "Leave him alone." He wrapped his arms around her. "How about Jay tells your mother we're heading out to my place and we get out of here?"

"I haven't finished my homework."

Kade laughed softly. "Do it Sunday night. Or Rian can do it. Come on. Let's get you out of here."

"They're in the kitchen."

"I'll head down and distract them. You can follow shortly." Jasper strode across the room.

Weariness washed over her and she sagged against Kade. She needed sleep. Desperately. She could hear Rian close down her laptop and ready her bag. Then Kade pulled away from her.

"Your brother is ready for you to leave now." Kade guided her to the door.

Rian handed her an overnight bag and Amber took it without a word as she left her room. Reaching the stairs, she paused at the top before slowly walking down. Avoiding looking at her mother and grandmother, she stopped at Jasper's side.

"We'll see you Sunday night. And quit worrying, Mum." Jasper guided her out to his car, opening the front passenger door for her. "Come on. Before Mum is out here with last minute instructions."

The front door opened as if Jasper's words had conjured her and Amber hastily sat and buckled herself in. Jasper strode around the front of his car, a wave and a smile for his mother. Within minutes they were on the road.

Amber glanced up as she sensed Kade and Rian overhead, Shannon's two warriors flanking them. She closed her eyes and fell asleep to be woken as they pulled up in front of Kade's house. Keeping her eyes closed, she tried to banish the sea of blood from her mind. She couldn't sleep without dreaming of it. No matter how short a sleep it was.

When she sensed Kade beside the car door, Amber opened it. She wearily hopped out and stared at him. He reached out and ran the back of his fingers along her cheekbone.

"Would sleeping tablets help?" Jasper asked from behind her.

Amber spun to face him. "No!" She couldn't think of anything worse than being trapped in her nightmares.

"It's okay. It was just a suggestion." He held his hands up as if to surrender.

Ronan walked towards them out of the Void.

"What have you done to yourself?" He stopped in front of Amber. "Chait, get out of the Void now." The Gold Dragon appeared beside Ronan in human form. Ronan turned to him, his eyes ice. "Why didn't you tell me? You said she was having trouble sleeping. She looks like the walking dead. You're meant to look out for her. Get out of my sight."

Chait did the smart thing and re-entered the Void.

"It's not his fault I can't sleep," Amber protested.

"Inside. I'm not standing out here to discuss this." Ronan looked towards Jasper. "Or anything else for that matter."

Amber trailed behind Ronan, Kade's arm around her waist. She dropped onto one of the kitchen chairs Rian held out for her and watched as Ronan placed six jewels on the table. He turned to Jasper.

"Do any of them look different to you?"

Jasper picked up two of them. "These two. They seem to be-"

"Keep your observations to yourself." Ronan turned to Amber. "You go and get some sleep before you collapse." He turned to Jasper again. "And you, follow me." He led the way to the bathroom and turned on the shower.

Amber had already told Jasper about running water

so he knew why Ronan wished to see him in the bathroom. He had secrets to share.

"Come on Amber." Kade rose to his feet. "Come and have a sleep."

She shook her head, her mind still filled with visions of blood.

"Then at least lie down and rest."

"I don't want to sleep," Amber muttered.

Kade pulled her to her feet. "Then rest. Just lie down and rest."

She didn't have the energy to argue so she let him lead her to his room. The curtains were closed and the room was in darkness. Dropping onto the bed, she stared up at the ceiling. She didn't want to sleep, but exhaustion claimed her and she once again fell into nightmares. She struggled to leave them, but something forced her to stay asleep.

"Quit trying to wake up."

Amber was shocked to hear Ronan's voice in her dream. "What are you doing here?"

"Sleep. You won't dream now."

"How do you know?" Amber could only see blackness. "Anything could be hidden in the dark."

"You're very difficult to please you know."

Amber smiled as her dream world lightened to a

rugged coastline with a sheer drop to jagged rocks in the ocean below. "Where is this place?"

"Home."

Amber turned to see Ronan seated beside her on the cliff, his legs hanging over the edge. And it was the real Ronan, right down to the gold flecks in his eyes. "I don't have a home."

"Mine."

"Where is it?"

"Shut up and rest, Amber." Ronan pointed behind her. "There's your bed. Now go and sleep in it."

A hand carved wooden bed sat on the rocky ground behind her. In the distance a castle rose above everything. It made the one they had stayed in look like a cottage. She turned back to Ronan who continued to look out to sea. "Is this your lands? The ones you want to get back?"

He nodded. "This is where I was born. I helped build that castle. Right where the hovel I was born in stood."

Amber met his gaze for a moment and then walked to the bed and curled up in it. The sound of waves lulled her to sleep and no cries of help invaded her dreams.

Chapter Nineteen

Amber slowly woke, stretching. She glanced around Kade's room and saw Ronan on the floor at the foot of the bed, his back against the wall as he watched her. The room was empty. Unless his Gold Dragon was in there too, but somehow she didn't think so.

"Where is everyone?"

"I chased them out last night."

"Why?" Amber slid over the end of the bed and onto the floor. She shuffled across the floor until she could lean up against the wall near Ronan. It reminded her of when they'd been in the dungeon together. She shied away from that thought.

"They annoyed me."

Amber smiled. It was probably more likely he hadn't wanted them to see him help her. "Why can't they do what you did?"

"They're too weak."

"Thank-"

"Shut up, Amber."

She laughed. It sounded like she wasn't the only one who got cranky when they had no sleep. Ronan rose to his feet, holding out a hand. Amber stared at it a moment before she took it and allowed him to pull her to her feet.

When Ronan started to release her hand, she tightened her grip. "I saw you last night. No illusions. Why?"

"It's easier." He pulled out of her grasp.

"About Jay-"

"He can see. But this doesn't release you from your vow. You cannot tell anyone else."

Amber nodded. But at least she had someone she could share it with.

"And give him something you've filled. He drew on the two I brought with me. I'm curious to see if he can do the same with yours." Ronan flung the bedroom door open and glared at Rian who stood there. "Do you always have to be underfoot?"

Rian ignored Ronan to run his gaze over Amber. He smiled. "You look rested."

"I feel it." It was the first time in days that she'd felt like smiling from happiness. "And I'm starved."

"There are fresh pikelets in the kitchen."

Ronan shook his head. "I never received such devotion when you served me."

"I guess it is true when they say having the right boss makes all the difference." Rian turned towards the kitchen.

Amber giggled as she glanced up at Ronan. "Don't worry, I'm sure I can manage to share a couple of them with you." She linked her arm through his.

"That's an annoying habit you have." He pulled away from her.

"Should I wait next time so you can check me over for weapons before I enter your personal space?"

"Don't push it." He strode towards the kitchen.

Amber followed. She was in a good mood and almost danced down the hallway to the kitchen. There were two plates of pikelets on the table. Butter, syrup and jam in the middle. Amber sat in front of one of the plates and waited until Ronan was also seated. "Thank you."

"I didn't do it for you." Ronan scraped a knife across the butter. "You're part of my plan. You need to be alert if we're going to pull it off."

Amber's good mood evaporated. The last thing she wanted to do was face Paili. Which was exactly why she needed to. "Do you have a plan?"

"Nearly. I'll let you know when it's completely

sorted." He slathered jam on the pikelet and popped it in his mouth. He gestured towards her plate. "Eat. You still look like crap."

"Thanks. That's just what I needed to hear."

Ronan grinned. "You're welcome."

She laughed and shook her head at Ronan's questioning look. Only Ronan would complain at genuine thanks and yet accept that which was given heavily laden with sarcasm.

Jasper and Kade entered the kitchen as she pushed her plate away and she sent a look to Rian, guessing he was the reason for such perfect timing. He ignored her look and cleared the table.

Kade sat down beside her. "You look a lot better."

Amber sent a glance to Ronan. "Really? I've been told I still look like crap." She slid one of her gold bracelets off, pushing it across the table to Jasper as he sat down.

"I don't think it's my style." Jasper drew the power from it then slid it back to her.

Amber smiled. "You sure? I was even going to throw in a flowery hair comb and some pink laced sandals to go with it."

"Oh well, now you're talking. If you add a floral dress and a bottle of pink nail polish you might have me convinced." Jasper grinned.

"Sorry, no floral dress."

Jasper shrugged. "Guess it's a no sale then."

Kade linked his fingers with Amber's. "You sound more rested too."

Before Amber could answer, Ronan rose to his feet. "I'll see you tonight." He vanished into the Void without another word.

"I hate when they do that," Jasper complained.

"Why? Because you think they're standing around waiting to see what you might say about them?" Amber grinned when her brother shrugged. She pushed away from the table. "Have we got anything planned for the day?"

Jasper shook his head. "Not that I know of, but I do need to talk to you for a few minutes. We could take a walk."

"If you don't need my company, I've got some things to do." Kade gave Amber a quick kiss when she shook her head.

Jasper headed for the back door, Amber at his side. He draped an arm around her shoulders. Rian followed a few metres behind as they silently headed through the long grass. Amber leaned her head back and breathed in deep, the scents bombarding her. The crisp air filled her lungs, soil mingled with the smell of prey. The panther in her stirred sleepily but she was well fed and settled down with no trouble. Amber recalled her first moment as a panther in this very place. She looked around with a slight smile on her lips.

"You look heaps better than you did yesterday." Jasper tapped under one of her eyes with the tip of his forefinger. "There's still smudges but you've lost that skeletal head look."

"I think you better go light on the compliments today. I don't think I could take any more without becoming completely conceited." Amber pulled away from her brother to hold out her arms and spin around. She grinned. "I always loved doing this on a winter's day when I was little."

Jasper smiled. "You and Crystal would hold hands and spin until you'd drop in the grass." He sobered. "Flinn has been making us train with his warriors. All of us in human form."

"What do you mean, train?"

"He thinks it'll only be a matter of time before there are other Dragon Mages. I know we tried to keep most of the process from Shannon, but she's not stupid. And neither is Ronan. One of them is sure to figure it out eventually."

Amber shrugged. "So? Then we won't be such a rarity. Surely that'll be a good thing."

"I wouldn't have a clue. But have you ever stopped to wonder why they decided not to have Dragon Mages? All records of them were removed and they stopped making them. Either let them die out or killed them. There must have been a reason."

Amber stared at Jasper. She'd never thought about it, but he was right. There had to have been some reason. "I'll ask Ronan. Maybe he knows."

"Possibly. But anyway, I was telling you about the training Flinn's making us do."

Amber nodded.

"He has us throw fire and ice at them."

"What! That's cruel. Jasper, don't tell me you go along with it."

"They don't just stand there and wait for us to hit them." He grinned. "It's training. They love it. Especially when we miss them. But, a couple of times when Crystal and I have hit them at the same time, they turn into dragons. They can't hold their human form."

"Because they are hit with ice and fire or because they are hit so much?"

Jasper shrugged. "That's what we're wondering." He glanced towards Rian.

Amber realised what he was leading up to. "No. Absolutely not."

Rian stepped forward. "It makes sense."

"I'm not attacking you."

Rian smiled momentarily. "You have before."

"That was different. You were trying to avoid being hit."

"You can heal me afterwards."

Amber glared at Rian. "Are you crazy?"

"No. Which is why we will do this."

"Why?"

"What if other mages are made? We need to know what to expect."

Amber's good mood evaporated. Why couldn't they have let her coast through the morning without dumping problems on her? She turned to glare at her brother. "This is your fault."

Jasper grinned. "Do I take it that's a yes?"

"Just don't hurt him."

Rian laughed. "You will both be throwing balls of fire at me. I can withstand a fair amount of fire being a dragon, but it still hits harder than a punch."

Amber sent him a daggered look. "Let's get this over with."

Rian nodded then walked a distance from them. He stood there, hands at his side, his sandy blond hair tied at the nape of his neck, the cold breeze playing with the ends. He wore dragon-leather pants and vest, the cold not seeming to bother him. He nodded once to let them know he was ready.

Amber was far from ready. A week of seeing Rian's body floating in a bloody sea, along with everyone else she cared for, made it even harder. Amber was jolted away from her thoughts when Jasper dropped a hand on her shoulder. She looked over at him.

"Waiting is even worse. Count of three?"

She lifted her hands, fire pooling in them as she did. Rian remained still, expressionless. She forced herself not to think of what it would feel like to have balls of fire impact with your body. *"One, two, three."* They launched the fireballs together. Amber winced as Rian staggered but stayed human.

Rian straightened. "Close. Try several each." He paused. "Better make that half a dozen." He grinned fleetingly. "But you can stop if I turn dragon."

Ronan emerged from the Void near Amber. She jumped back, glaring at him. "A little warning would be nice."

"That's what I was thinking." Ronan gestured towards Rian. "I would have stuck around longer if I'd known how entertaining the day was going to be."

"Ronan, he's your son."

Ronan grinned. "I know. That's why I expect more

of him than other warriors. Now, this time aim for the heart. That should make it harder for him to hold his form."

Amber turned to Jasper who nodded, fireballs in his hands. She looked across the paddock to Rian who waited. He gave a single nod. *"Heart?"* Amber began to think Rian wouldn't reply, but he widened his stance and inclined his head again.

"Heart on three." Amber stared at Rian, her arms at her side. *"One, two, three."* She raised her hands, fireballs forming as she said three. The moment she flung them at Rian, she rapidly sent more at him. He stood steady through three impacts, the fourth causing him to become a dragon. She lowered her hands, ignoring the slight tremble in them. It was one thing to attack wyverns, another to face a friend. She started towards Rian who roared in pain, clawing at the ground. Ronan grabbed her upper arm.

Amber tried to pull free. "He's hurt."

Kade, Brann and Maira came flying in. They landed near Amber, becoming human.

Ronan tightened his grip. "Wait."

Amber stared into his eyes, wishing she was stronger. She was tempted to throw a fireball at his heart.

Ronan grinned. "Maybe one day."

Amber was confused. Surely he didn't know what she had wanted to do. Although, maybe he did. But why would he let her throw fireballs at him? She shook her head, too confused. "Let me help him." She ignored the discussion behind her between Kade and Jasper. "Let me go. You're hurting me."

"Then stop struggling." Ronan's grip tightened when Rian roared, took flight and landed near them. "And shut up. You're stirring him up."

"Then let me go."

"Amber, talk to Rian before you try and heal him," Kade said from behind her.

She reached out with her mind and hit a wall of anger and pain. She couldn't reach Rian. It was almost like trying to contact a wyvern. She stopped struggling. "Jay?"

He shook his head. "Flinn's warriors weren't like that, but they didn't last as long as Rian either."

"Of course not." Derision filled Ronan's voice. "There's not a single bit of Gold in their ancestors."

"Will he be all right?" Amber asked Ronan.

Ronan let her go. "Give him time."

Amber took a couple of steps towards Rian who no longer tried to tear at the ground. He stood menacingly in front of them as if ready to attack. She took another couple of steps. "Rian. Lie down."

She kept her voice firm. The fear she felt was pushed aside. Minutes passed before he pressed himself against the ground. She stepped closer, stopping when he growled. "Stay still. Be quiet." She kept her orders simple. Another couple of steps and she pressed her hands against his scales. She drew the pain from him, healing his wounds. He became human beneath her hands and she knelt on the ground to continue healing him.

Rian tried to push her away. "Enough. Do not wear yourself out on me."

Amber threw her arms around him, drawing energy from one of her gold bracelets as she did. "You worried me." She finished healing him.

"I did not last long. I think I need more practice. It was all I could do to stop myself from attacking you." Rian grinned at Amber's shocked expression.

She pushed him hard enough he landed in the dirt on his back. "You're an idiot."

Chapter Twenty

Rian laughed as Amber rose to her feet and stalked away from him. His laughter faded as Ronan stood over him. Amber spun and stopped, ready to come to Rian's defence if he needed it. Ronan held out his hand. Rian stared at his father a moment before he took the hand and allowed himself to be pulled to his feet. Amber continued to watch them warily.

Ronan stared at Rian. "We can use this." He stepped back, raising his voice. "All of you. Out of the Void." Six Gold Warriors answered his call and came forward to stand behind Rian. Ronan eyed them all as they continued to stand at attention.

"What are you planning, Ronan?" Amber started to walk back to him.

"We need to see how long Golds last."

"You are not exhausting her," Rian stated.

Ronan looked over at Amber. "Are you exhausted?"

She shook her head. He knew perfectly well she had extra stores to draw on these days. But that didn't mean she was going to use them all. She needed some for reserves.

Kade came to stand beside her, Brann at his heels, Maira off to the side. "You don't have to do this if you don't want, Amber. You're entitled to a day of rest."

"She had rest. An entire night of it." Ronan met Amber's gaze.

She waited for him to point out it was because of him she'd slept, but he didn't. Amber smiled. "I don't mind using up some extra energy if I know I can look forward to another restful night."

With a nod, Ronan grinned. "We might make a dragon of you yet." He turned to his warriors. "You," he pointed to the one that looked the oldest. "And you." The second warrior's eyes were almost pure gold in colour, even in his human form. "The rest of you become dragons. Keep them from doing anything stupid when they turn."

The golden-eyed warrior asked, "What makes you think they can force a Gold to change?"

"What makes you think they can't, Alsandair?"

"Rian barely has any Gold. Flinn's warriors have none at all."

"How much extra Gold would there be in your veins compared to my son? Sixteen times more? Thirty-two?"

Alsandair shrugged. "Possibly more."

Ronan smiled. He looked like a predator about to pounce on a meal. "How about I be real nice. Rian lasted four hits. Why don't we double that? You last eight hits and you get a bonus."

"How much?"

Ronan turned to Amber. "What was your hawk weight in gold again?"

"About half a kilo." She smiled as she recalled the last time she'd made that comment.

"What do you think, Amber? Will he be a dragon in eight hits? Is he stronger than your warrior?"

Amber laughed. She knew Ronan was deliberately encouraging her competitive streak. As well as insulting her through his insinuations that Rian was weak. "I guess we'll soon see. If he thinks he's up to it. No reluctant volunteers." She strode forward to stand at Ronan's side. "Well, Alsandair?"

"Exactly the same treatment you gave your own warrior," Alsandair said.

Amber nodded. "Straight at the heart."

Alsandair held out his hand and Amber shook it. He turned and walked across the paddock to stop the same distance from her that Rian had stood. Amber glanced towards Kade when he momentarily rested his hand on her shoulder. Jasper came to stand on the other side of her as everyone moved from between her and Alsandair.

"Are you up to this?" Amber held out her wrist in front of Jasper, palm up, offering him some of the power stored in her gold bracelets.

"No problems." He pushed her arm away. "Count of three?"

Amber grinned as she brought her hands up, flames ready. She stared at Alsandair's heart. *"One, two, three."* They rapidly threw balls of fire at Alsandair who staggered at the third one and burst into dragon form at the fifth attack.

With a roar, he flew at them. All the other dragons launched into the air, Kade and Ronan included. Jasper threw his hands up as if to protect himself and Amber started to throw more fireballs. Instead of flames coming from Jasper, it seemed like a rush of air and sound travelled through the air and all airborne dragons crashed into the ground becoming human except for Alsandair. Jasper collapsed on the ground and Amber threw herself at him. She grabbed his hand to wrap it around one of her gold bracelets.

"All of it." She spoke the words only to Jasper, breathing a sigh of relief as he pulled her power into himself.

"What the hell was that?" Jasper ran a shaky hand through his hair.

Kade picked himself up off the ground, waving Brann and Maira back. He dusted himself off. "Whatever it was, it packed a hell of a punch."

Ronan was already on his feet glaring at his warriors as they stumbled to their feet. "Shake it off, girls. A stiff breeze would knock you off your feet right now." He gestured towards Alsandair who was still a dragon, struggling to make his limbs work as he snarled and growled. "And someone deal with him."

The five warriors turned dragon again and restrained Alsandair. Amber ran across the ground and healed the wounded dragon enough to allow him to become human. He waved her off before he was completely healed.

"I have the energy to complete the healing," Amber told him. She drew power from one of the jewels in her plaited dragon-leather bracelet while she waited for his answer. He looked over towards Ronan. She guessed he was given permission when he nodded.

Alsandair took her hand when she was finished. "It was unnecessary. Thank you, mage. And I concede the win to you," he glanced towards Rian, "And your warrior."

"But you outlasted him."

"I have five years more experience and a lot more strength from being Gold. I barely made it to the fifth hit. You nearly had me at the third. It was a dismal effort." He pulled a business card from his black, dragon-leather jacket. "My current service has three more months. Call me if you ever need a Gold Dragon."

Amber took the card, staring at it in surprise.

"Stop trying to steal all my warriors," Ronan growled from beside her. "You've got one more Gold to turn dragon." He looked at his warriors who argued amongst themselves. "Once they figure out who gets the honour."

"Honour!" Amber stared at Ronan, certain he must be joking.

Kade laughed as he joined them. "And you thought you were competitive."

"Oh, of all the idiotic–" she broke off, unable to think of something strong enough to say. She growled instead.

"Survival of–" Kade started to say.

Amber elbowed him in the ribs. "Oh shut up."

"I will see to lunch while you finish off your game," Rian said.

"That's not why I'm annoyed," Amber said.

"Okay." Rian's tone showed he clearly didn't believe. He exchanged a look with Kade who nodded and then strode back to the house.

"I can look after myself," Amber muttered, guessing at what they'd probably said to each other.

Kade smiled. "I know. But it never hurts to have someone at your back. An ally you can trust."

Before Amber could answer, one of the Golds strode over to them and she guessed a decision had been reached. She was tempted to ask how he'd earned the 'honour' but decided she didn't really want to know. He walked out the correct distance then turned and faced them, waiting.

Amber turned to Jasper. "Are you up to it again?"

He nodded. "As long as I don't go doing anything like last time." He grinned. "At this rate I'm going to have to start wearing my jocks on the outside."

Amber laughed. "You're not as good looking as a superhero so I don't think you could carry it off."

"That won't be a problem. I'll just wear a mask." Jasper raised his hands. "Count of three?"

Amber nodded and faced the warrior who waited

for them. *"One, two, three."* He lasted four attacks and then he was mobbed by all the other dragons who struggled to restrain him. It took nearly twenty minutes until he was subdued enough for Amber to heal him. Then Ronan had her attack two of his warriors, to see if repeated attacks from one mage did the same as attacks from two. After she'd attacked them two dozen times each, nothing had happened. Other than she'd needed to heal them.

Ronan stared thoughtfully at his warriors. "A couple of Gold Warriors that were forced into turning dragon amongst our enemies might be useful."

"All I could think of was to kill," Alsandair said. "I didn't care who I killed, friend or foe." The other man who'd earned the honour of being forced into dragon form nodded in agreement.

"Rian said he was able to stop himself from attacking me. Barely," Amber said.

"It seems like the more Gold in their line, the more they were affected," Kade said.

"I wonder if the ice and fire combination causes a different result. Or the ice and fire combination of different mages." Ronan looked between Amber and Jasper.

"Forget it." Kade draped an arm around Amber. "Time for a break. And lunch."

Ronan looked like he was about to argue. Then he turned to his warriors. "Back to the Void." They instantly disappeared. He faced Amber. "What time do you go to bed?"

"You mean you haven't been given that intel yet?"

"Don't be annoying, Amber."

She couldn't resist smiling at him. "Probably nine tonight."

He nodded before he vanished into the Void.

Amber walked at Kade's side, a little tired. Jasper and Brann walked ahead of them, quietly talking. She did a quick search with her mind and found Maira in the house with Rian and Shannon's warriors, who still guarded Jasper from a distance. She hoped it wasn't too big a distance if trouble came, but with Jasper's new ability it looked like he could take care of himself better than any dragon. But he did need to learn how to store power to draw on if he was going to use that ability.

"Jay." Amber waited until he turned to look at her, pausing at the back door. "How do you feel about wearing an earring?" She grinned at his look of confusion and touched her blood red teardrop that hung from her right ear.

"Not that one." Jasper stepped out of the doorway so she and Kade could enter the house.

"This one is mine. What about a plain gold sleeper?" Amber sat at the kitchen table, taking a drink from the glass of juice that sat near her plate of medium cooked steak.

"That'd be bearable."

Amber turned to Rian who stood behind her chair. "Can you bring me back the two sleepers that are on my duchess?"

"Hey, I never agreed to have two. And who's going to pierce them?" Jasper demanded.

Maira moved close to Jasper, tugging on his ear. "I've pierced things before." She grinned.

"Did they live through the experience?"

Maira laughed at Jasper's question. "Is that an issue?"

Chapter Twenty-One

After lunch, Jasper reluctantly let Maira pierce his ear with a needle and Amber took the pain from it during the procedure. Since he'd only allow them to do one piercing, Amber snapped the other sleeper closed over the first so they were linked together like a chain. She then turned to Kade.

"Have you got any drinking glasses you don't want?"

Kade gestured towards the cupboard. "I'm not attached to any of them."

"Just don't leave us without coffee cups," Maira said.

Amber gathered a handful of glasses and retreated to the bathroom with Jasper. She showed him how she'd learned to fill them with her power and grinned as he ended up smashing every one of them. She turned on the shower so they could speak privately.

"I have a handful of jewels Ronan gave me that I didn't break. You can have them. But it might be best to try on different things. I found gold to be really good to work with. But that doesn't mean you will. And I'll get Ronan to have some jewellery made for you. Something you like better than these." Amber rattled her gold bracelets.

"I can't understand why he won't let us tell Crystal."

Amber nodded. "I know. But maybe one day we can talk him into it."

"Forget about we, it's you he likes."

"Yeah, but I think some days the only thing he likes about me is that he'd like to rip out my heart."

"You do tend to have that kind of effect on people sometimes."

"Only parents, teachers, and people who can make my life miserable."

Jasper fiddled with his new earring. "I've been thinking of moving out of home. Dad is full of questions about what I'm up to. Am I going out too much, who are the strange people visiting and are they in a gang?"

Amber laughed. "That was one of my first questions I asked them."

"It's all the leather. And he's started lecturing me

since I've been wearing dragon-leather pants. It's just a hassle. Besides, I earned a bit over sixteen thousand from helping Shannon with the wyvern nest. I'm sure I can earn more."

"I've got a house somewhere you can stay in."

"What do you mean, somewhere?"

"Rian is anticipating I'll leave home next year. If you move there first I can tell them I'm moving in with you."

"Who owns the house?"

Amber shrugged. "I don't know."

"It isn't Ronan, is it? You don't want to be any further in his debt."

Amber searched for Rian and found him outside the bathroom. She opened the door, motioning him in. "Who owns the house?"

Rian closed the door behind him. "What house?"

"Where I'll stay next year."

"You do."

"What? How's that possible? I don't have that kind of money. What have you done, Rian?"

"Made Ronan pay for your services up front. Do not expect any more from him once you help him get his lands back."

"Am I even old enough to own property? I'm only seventeen."

Rian shrugged. "I do not know. It is owned by a company that is owned by a trust of which you are the sole beneficiary. It is the way Ronan organises his dealings in this world. Except there are many more layers of companies and businesses before you find the owner."

"Is it big enough for Jay to stay there?"

Rian grinned momentarily. "Maybe we should make time for you to see it."

"Please tell me it's not some kind of mansion."

"If that is what you wish."

Jasper laughed. "So what do Crystal and I get paid if Amber gets a mansion?"

"She also received a discovery fee. Without her, you two would not be mages."

Amber sat on the edge of the bathtub. "This is all too much. I don't need a mansion."

"It is not a mansion, Amber. There are only five bedrooms."

"Than what is it?"

"Spacious."

"I want to see it."

"Tomorrow. If you get enough sleep tonight," Rian said.

Amber glared at him. "You're not my mother."

"No, I am worse." He grinned fleetingly. "I am your first warrior."

Jasper laughed again.

"Oh, leave me alone. The pair of you." She pointed to the door, glaring at them until they left the bathroom. She turned off the water and sat on the floor with her back against the wall. A knock on the door had her searching out who was on the other side. It was Kade. She was tempted to tell him to go away too. She sighed. She must be getting tired again since she didn't have a reason to be mad at Kade. And no wonder, with all she'd done today.

"Amber?"

She stared at the door. "Oh fine. Come in."

Kade sat beside her once he closed the door. He slid an arm around her shoulders and sat quietly.

She rested her head against him, closing her eyes for a moment. Nine o'clock was going to be a long time coming, but she didn't dare have a nap before then. She couldn't face another nightmare. "Do you think it'll take Ronan much longer to sort out a plan?"

"I don't know. But I think it's more than figuring out a plan. It always is with Ronan."

"What else is there?"

Kade shrugged. "Your guess is as good as mine.

But, whatever it is you can bet there are going to be some very unhappy people as a result."

* * *

After a restful night, courtesy of Ronan, Amber convinced Rian she was up to a trip to the city. Which meant Kade and his warriors had to join her. And of course Jasper didn't want to be left out. He called in on his mother and told her he was leaving early but Amber would stay the day with Maira and be back before bed. It didn't take him too long to convince her to let Amber have the rest of the day out and then they headed to the city. Jasper picked them up at the park they waited at, since having them in his car would have ruined his explanation. As there weren't enough seats, Brann volunteered to fly, carrying a saddle for the return flight.

By the time they reached the city, four hours later, Amber began to wish she'd flown. She'd never been a good traveller. The long hours of sitting made her feel bored and restless. Rian started to direct Jasper once they reached the city. Eventually, they pulled up at a concrete and iron gate and Rian got out to put a pin number into the panel on the gatepost by the driver's door.

Amber watched as the gates slowly swung open and Jasper drove up the paved drive. Amber stared suspiciously at the house. It didn't seem too big a house from the front. Well, not large enough to be a mansion, but it did have a covered area at the door where a car could stop if it rained. Rian handed Amber a key and gestured to the front door.

She stopped in front of it, worried what she might find behind the large double doors. There was another keypad beside the front door and Rian told her the pin number in her mind. Once they entered, he showed them around. Past a spare room, off to the left, there was a suite of two rooms for Doneele and the woman she called granny. The master suite contained a study and exercise room as well as two walk-in closets and a sitting room. And although Rian had told her the truth, there were only five bedrooms, he had left out the fact that each had its own bathroom and there was a dining and breakfast room as well as a living and family room. A covered patio led out to a swimming pool where Maira and Brann took advantage of the heated water. Jasper remained in the room that overlooked the swimming pool trying to decide where all his gear would go while Amber paced the fully furnished master bedroom. Kade lay on the king-sized bed, his hands behind his head as he watched her.

Rian stood by the doors that led onto the covered patio his gaze following Amber as she muttered and complained while she paced. "This isn't me. I want something-" she growled. "Less. This is overkill. How am I meant to live here? I'd be worried about spilling something and ruining the carpets." She stopped to glare at Rian. "Are you going to say something or do you plan on just standing there all day?"

"I chose it because of the security system. There are motion cameras, coded entrances, security screens and it is well fenced. I wanted you to feel safe."

At Rian's words, Amber sagged on the bed beside Kade. She wanted to feel safe too. Now she felt like an idiot. "Thank you, Rian."

Kade tugged her to him. "Can we all stop running for cover now?"

Amber smiled wryly. "It's still not me."

"We can buy furniture from the op-shop if that'll help," Kade suggested.

Humour touched Amber's smile. "I know. I'm being an idiot."

Kade half sat up so he leaned over her. "You'll get used to it. It'll just take you time."

"Hey, Amber." Jasper knocked on the door that led to the patio.

Amber pushed Kade away so she could sit up and look at her brother through the glass door. "What?"

"How am I going to convince Dad I can afford to live here?"

"I have a suggestion," Rian said.

"Go ahead. I wouldn't have a clue," Amber said.

"Isleen is giving you room and board in exchange for taking care of the yard and pool," Rian said.

"Who's Isleen?" Amber asked.

"The housekeeper."

"Oh." Amber had never heard her called anything other than Doneele's granny. "Where are they?"

"They are giving you time to have a look around before they return." Rian glanced at his watch. "They will be back in about a quarter of an hour."

"So when can I move in?" Jasper asked.

Amber grinned at her brother. "Whenever you want. But just remember, our parents will probably blame you when I move in here." She turned to Rian. "And how are you going to explain that? Not to mention this being my room."

"The story is that Isleen lost her husband several

years ago and cannot bear to sleep in here now as this was their room. She cannot afford the people to maintain this place, but her husband bought it for her as a wedding gift so she does not wish to part with it. And Doneele is her husband's daughter. He was much older than her," Rian said.

When Isleen arrived, Amber saw why Rian said Doneele was to be her husband's child. There was no way the woman could have passed as anyone's granny, let alone a thirteen-year-old's mother. She had long black hair tightly plaited in a single strand down her back, blue eyes that were almost violet, was petite and looked to be barely in her mid twenties.

Isleen strode towards Amber who rose from the lounge chair in the living room where she'd waited for them to arrive. "I am pleased to finally meet you. I hope everything is suitable. Let me know if you would like any changes made."

Amber took Isleen's hand and wished she didn't feel so lost for words. This woman was meant to be her housekeeper? She was so not ready for this. "The house looks lovely." What else could she say? It was far too impressive for her to live in? Instead Amber turned to Doneele. She was relieved to see the girl didn't look the least like her father. She had bright red hair, blue eyes, freckled skin and a mischievous grin.

Amber wondered if she knew what had happened to her father.

"Granny tried to teach me how to curtsey to you, but I'd probably land on you if I attempted it."

Amber grinned, holding out her hand. "We'll stick with a handshake then."

"Doni, you need to remember to call me Isleen now."

Doneele shook Amber's hand and turned to Isleen. "I know. But it takes time. I can't remember everything all at once. There's a million stories I have to keep straight."

"You are a Gold Dragon, it should be second nature for you to keep them straight," Isleen said.

"Yeah, okay." Doneele turned back to Amber. "Can I have a TV in my room? Aren't they awesome? All the kids at my school have their own TV and laptop. Can I have one of them too?"

"Doneele! Enough." Isleen grabbed the girl by her shoulders, pushing Doneele behind her. The girl was nearly as tall as her. "She does not mean to be ungrateful."

Amber managed to prevent the smile that wanted to escape. *"Can I afford what she wants?"* She asked Rian who gave a slight nod. "Whatever you need to maintain normal appearances, Isleen."

"I do not know this world. It is very different from ours," Isleen said.

"Jay will be moving in soon. I'm sure he'll be able to help you figure it out," Amber said.

Jasper nodded. "Sure. Anything you need to know, just ask."

With the way Jasper looked at Isleen, she hoped she hadn't just created another problem for herself. *"She's way too old for you, brother."* Jasper grinned at her in answer.

Jasper took off early, after Rian had handed out keys and told him the pin numbers. He wanted to start moving in as soon as possible. Still feeling uncomfortable in her home, Amber rang Crystal hoping to catch up, but Flinn had other plans for the day. In the end, they left as soon as it started to grow dark. Kade was saddled with the one Brann had brought with him and Amber relaxed against him as they flew home. She didn't dare sleep. She'd wait until Ronan could keep the nightmares away.

Chapter Twenty-Two

They reached Helen's house well before they were expected and Amber found the place empty. Wanting some time alone, she sent Kade and his warriors home and slowly headed up the stairs towards her room. She paused at the top, staring at the two locked doors. They'd been bothering her for months. Her grandmother kept telling her they were none of her business. They probably weren't, but it was driving her crazy not to know.

She mentally searched for her grandmother and found her several houses away with a group of other people in a building. She guessed it was a house, but she couldn't sense inanimate objects that accurately. Just the impression of their solidness. Amber ranged further afield and found her mother in a building along the highway. A curl of anger started and Amber pushed it away. She couldn't afford to get angry.

Her mother was extremely close to someone and Amber could tell it was a man. A man who wasn't her father. How many more secrets did her mother have? And when had she planned to tell them? She was sick of secrets. People keeping them from her and having to keep them from other people.

Amber turned to Rian who patiently stood behind her on the stairs. "Can you pick this lock?" She gestured towards the locked door in front of her.

"Are you sure you really want to know what is behind this door?"

"I wouldn't have asked if I didn't." She moved out of the way so Rian could step ahead of her.

"Give me a minute." Rian entered her room and returned a moment later with a small bag of tools.

"What are they?"

"Shh." Rian used the tools to quickly unlock the first door, swinging it open and sliding his hand inside to turn on the light.

Amber stared open-mouthed at the room. She quickly turned the switch off, closing the door. "Lock it again."

Rian laughed softly. "Did you want me to unlock the other one?"

Amber shook her head and hurried into her bedroom. She dropped onto her bed and stared at the closed curtains that hid the French doors. What on earth was her grandmother doing with an armoury in a bedroom of her house? And not just any armoury, but what looked like a medieval one. She rose to her feet and started to pace. She wanted to demand answers, but she couldn't. Not without admitting to breaking into the room.

Rian closed her bedroom door and locked it. "Amber?"

She shook her head. She needed to think. Why would anyone have that type of gear? There were no medieval knights. Or were there? "What did it mean?"

Rian shrugged. "I can only guess. I do not know for certain."

"What would you guess?"

"That a Knight has lived here at some stage."

"As in a dragon killing knight?"

Rian nodded.

"But-" she didn't know how to word the question. "We're not in the Middle Ages anymore."

"They still exist. Although they usually have modern weapons, not the ancient ones in that room."

"But-" Amber's mind went blank.

"This town would have been chosen because a Knight lives here. Not necessarily in this house.

There would be no challenge to the test if at least one person in the town did not know dragons exist, and want to kill them if they discovered one."

Amber's legs could no longer support her and she dropped onto her bed. "Knights." She lay back, her feet still on the floor. "My mother has a boyfriend and my grandmother has an armoury. Just great."

"What boyfriend?" Rian asked.

Amber didn't answer. Why hadn't Kade told her how dangerous a year in her world was? Should he be flying in and out of her room at all hours? There was still just over five months left before the end of this test. The last day of the year. And that seemed like an impossibly long time to get through.

She continued to lie on her bed as first her grandmother came home, rummaged around in the kitchen and then headed off to her room and then her mother walked in the front door. Amber was seated at the table in the darkened kitchen when her mother entered.

"Where've you been?"

"Oh! Amber! You scared me. Why are you sitting in the dark?" Donna turned on the light.

Amber blinked, trying to accustom herself to the brightness. "Where have you been?"

"Out. I don't have to answer to you, Amber. Now

go and get ready for bed. You've got school tomorrow."

"Who is he?"

"Did you hear me, Amber?"

"I'm sitting right here and don't have the slightest hearing problem. So yeah, I'm guessing I heard you very clearly." Amber rose to her feet, pushing the panther back down. "Who was the man you were with tonight?"

"I'm not going to talk to you while you're behaving like this. If spending the weekend with your friends is going to result in this kind of behaviour then it might be best if you didn't spend so much time with them."

Amber took a step closer to Donna. "I can smell his cologne on you. What do you take me for? An idiot?"

"Like you sometimes think I am?"

"And what's that supposed to mean?"

"Why don't you admit it, Amber? What drugs are you on?"

Amber laughed sharply. "What do you want? Do you want me tested? I am not, nor have I ever been, on drugs. Shall we go now? Maybe they'll do the test at the hospital."

"I'm not in the mood for these theatrics, Amber."

"Then tell me who the hell you were with tonight. How hard is that?"

Helen appeared in the doorway. "Can't a person sleep around here? And give it up Donna. Even I can smell his cologne from way over here. What does he do? Drown himself in it?"

Donna sank onto a kitchen chair. "Why don't you ask your father about his girlfriend?"

Amber stared at her mother. "I'm over this. I'm staying at Maira's. At least she doesn't lie to me all the time."

"I didn't lie to you, I just didn't think you were up to hearing about it. Now go to your room, Amber. We'll talk about this when you're feeling more rational."

Amber felt a growl rumble up through her body and barely managed to hold it back. She could almost feel the panther. "No."

"If you do not get up to your room right now, I am coming down to get you, Amber," Rian warned.

She ignored him, continuing to glare at her mother. If she had moved even a centimetre she probably would have become a panther. "Jasper is leaving home. I can't see why I should have to stick around to put up with all this crap when he doesn't."

Donna rose to her feet. "Since when is he leaving home?"

"He told me this arve." She belatedly recalled she had supposedly not been with her brother. "When he rang me." She had to hold on a little longer.

"If you pair can manage to keep it down, I'm going back to sleep." They ignored Helen as she pushed away from the doorway.

"He can't leave home," Donna said.

"Why not? You did. And you dragged me with you. And I didn't even know we were leaving home."

"You're not still harping on about that are you?"

"I am serious, Amber. You are barely holding on. I can smell how close the panther is to escaping. What will your mother say if you turn into a panther?"

"Obviously I'm still harping on about it. But only because you're still lying to me about stuff."

"If you could handle things a lot better we might bother to tell you about them." A knock on the front door interrupted Donna. "You go to your bed while I answer the door." She turned away.

Amber opened her mouth to say no, but Rian's hand prevented her as he picked her up and headed up the stairs. She struggled, trying to get away from him. They were barely in her room with the door closed when Amber lost control and became a panther. She turned on Rian, sinking her teeth into his leg. As blood filled her mouth, she came to her senses, turning human again. Running to the bathroom, she rinsed her mouth. When she finished, she looked up to see Rian watched her warily from the doorway.

"Sorry." She knelt beside him to heal his leg. "I don't know…" her words trailed off and she rested her head against the doorway.

"I should have made sure you ate as soon as we arrived home."

Amber smiled slightly. "I just…" she closed her eyes. She had let it all get to her. She should know better than that by now and not let anger take over. "Who was at the door?"

"I sent the Gold."

"Don't tell me I missed all the fun."

Amber opened her eyes to see that Ronan stood near Rian, eyeing his leg. "I guess you'll just have to learn to arrive earlier."

Ronan smiled, holding a hand out to Amber as Rian started to clean the blood off the timber floor. Amber allowed Ronan to help her up. She strode across the room and walked outside to lean on the rail of her small balcony. Ronan followed.

"Why would someone have an armoury?"

"What type of armoury?"

Amber turned slightly so she could watch Ronan's expression. "A medieval one."

"They're a collector? A re-enactor?"

"Does my grandmother look like either one?"

"Do you mean to say you think only a certain type of person can be a collector or re-enactor? How narrow minded of you, Amber."

"Stop playing with words, Ronan. Tell me what you know."

"You could try asking your grandmother."

"And have her know I broke into one of her locked rooms?"

Ronan grinned. "Only one? Did you chicken out, Amber?"

She pushed away from the rail. "I'm tired."

"Yes, that would probably help to explain the mood you're in tonight."

Amber ignored the comment and strode inside. She paused when she saw a hot cup of soup on her bedside drawers. A glance at Rian showed he was his usual expressionless self. She was tempted to apologise again, but didn't want to hear any comment Ronan might make about her attacking his son.

Sitting on the edge of her bed, she drank half her soup. She didn't feel like food. Not after trying to make a meal out of Rian. Handing the cup to Rian, she lay down, turning off her lamp. Rian headed to the balcony and Amber guessed Ronan had chased him out. Ronan sat on the bed, his back against the wall at the head of her bed.

She mentally searched the area. "Where's Kade?"

"I sent him home." Ronan looked over at her when she made no comment. "No complaints? Or are you getting sick of the boy?"

"I'm tired."

Ronan stared down at her. "Go to sleep. He said he'd pick you up in the morning. For school."

She met Ronan's steady gaze for several more minutes before she closed her eyes. Exhaustion claimed her. There was so much missed sleep she needed to catch up on. Not to mention she was back to putting power into everything around her again. She didn't want to be in a situation where she didn't have enough.

Chapter Twenty-Three

Wednesday lunchtime, Amber's phone rang as she sat near Kade, finishing her food. "I'm at school, Ronan. Can't it wait?"

"Time to make a move. I only really need you Amber, but I doubt your boys will let you go without them."

"I can't. I've still got classes this afternoon."

"Amber. I'm not asking. You have twenty minutes to get to Kade's house." Ronan disconnected.

Kade took her hand. "I guess you're about to get into some more trouble."

Amber sighed. "I'm going to get grounded again."

"We're experienced at dealing with that." Kade grinned. "Come on. Maira has the car ready and Brann and Rian are in it."

When they reached the farm, it was to find Jasper there. He sat beside Ronan on a verandah rail, nodding his head as Ronan talked to him, falling silent as they approached.

Ronan rose when they all stopped in front of him. "I have enough Golds with me who know the shortcuts through the Void that we'll all end up where we need to be. The three Golds with Amber, Jasper and Rian will fly to the courtyard entrance and drop down there to become human. Amber and Jasper need to turn them into berserker dragons immediately. We need them for a diversion."

Amber grinned. "Berserker. It has a nice ring to it."

Ronan sent her a look that clearly said shut up. "Crystal will be with me informing me of every hidden Gold. To make it easier, our army are all wearing blue vests." Ronan clicked his fingers and warriors stepped out of the Void, dressed in blue vests and a variety of different coloured dragon-leather pants. "But if someone does attack you and they have on a blue vest, kill them. It's always possible someone from Paili's army randomly chose blue today."

"Do we have to wear blue too?" Amber asked.

"No. They all know what you look like." Ronan glanced at Amber's companions. "All of you."

"Other than a diversion, what's the rest of the plan?" Kade asked.

"To listen when I speak. Paili must die. I'll direct

with Crystal's help. Time to go." Ronan motioned his warriors forward.

"Wait a minute. You spent over a week coming up with that? Surely there's more to it than what you've told us," Amber said.

"Of course there is. Everyone has been briefed with the information they need to know. Now it's time to put it all together."

Amber shook her head. "How can we win with so little information given out?"

"Easily. Let's go." Ronan disappeared into the Void before Amber could ask another question.

"Great!"

Alsandair stepped in front of Amber, grinning at her comment. He held out his hand. "I would be honoured if you allowed me to lead you through the Void."

"I hate the Void." Amber took his hand anyway with a glance towards Rian who took the hand of another Gold. Suddenly Amber realised who was going to be a diversion. "Will you be okay? I mean, you're going to be attacking the enemy with only two other dragons."

Alsandair's grin stayed in place. "I can't wait."

Amber rolled her eyes. "Let's get this over with."

They were in the Void longer than she expected,

the air feeling like it was pressing in on her, and nausea nearly caused her to lose her lunch. She sank to the ground where they stood overlooking a castle, close enough that she could see the expressions on the faces of those who were on guard duty. None of them appeared to be expecting trouble. Amber, Jasper and Rian were hidden from view by a forested area, the Golds having returned to the Void.

Amber reached out with her mind. *"Kade?"*

"I'm nearby."

"Is everyone in place?" Ronan asked. There were various affirmative answers. Amber bet no one would be game to tell Ronan any different. *"Send in the distraction."*

Three Gold Dragons stepped out of the Void near Amber. Still sitting on the ground, she looked up, relieved it was allies.

Alsandair held out his hand, helping Amber to her feet. "Attack me first, then Chait," he gestured towards the Gold who often shadowed Amber. "Then Anrai." As soon as Amber and Jasper nodded, the three warriors took to the air and flew the short distance to the castle.

Amber watched as they landed, well away from each other, Paili's warriors taking to the air ready to attack them. "One, two three," Amber called out the moment the dragons became human. "Next!" Within seconds, the three men were dragons, wildly attacking anything that came near them.

Dragons flew in from four different directions, attacking the warriors that were stationed on the battlements and towers of the castle. Amber watched as chaos erupted. When Alsandair landed in the dirt, she started to move forward. Rian restrained her with a hand on her shoulder. She breathed a sigh of relief when Alsandair picked himself up, shook his head and launched himself into the air again.

"Amber, Jasper, fly in the front door," Ronan ordered. *"Rian, Kade, watch their backs. Amber check ahead before you enter. Warn if there is anyone."*

Amber took a deep breath and became a goshawk, her brother doing the same. She searched ahead, finding the entrance hall of the castle empty. Before she reached the large, timber doors that were open, Crystal darted in ahead of her.

"No surprises," Crystal said.

"Amber, find Paili," Ronan ordered.

She searched through the castle, her mind roaming from room to room. She felt a tug. Below. Paili was somewhere beneath her. *"Almost directly beneath my feet."*

Three dragons burst into the large entrance hall

and became Ronan, Kade and Rian as they landed. Ronan ran towards one of the exits. *"Hurry up. Do you want her to escape?"*

Amber, Jasper and Crystal changed into their human forms and ran after him. Amber was glad of her ability to keep track of people with how quickly Ronan ran. They passed several groups of warriors fighting and Amber tried not to notice the unmoving dragons she occasionally saw, glad she didn't recognise any of them.

Ronan led them down a level and four dragons appeared ahead of him. "Jasper! Now!" Ronan threw himself on the floor and Jasper leapt ahead of them, throwing up his hands. A rush of air and sound travelled through the air and the dragons were thrown against the far wall, becoming human.

Amber noticed for the first time that Jasper wore rings on his fingers. Ones that Ronan had asked her to fill with power yesterday. Jasper had drawn on the stored power as his own drained away. Ronan jumped to his feet and Amber turned away as he finished off the warriors. She wasn't good at this survival of the fittest stuff. Maybe losing her lunch earlier would have been preferable to the way she was feeling now.

Amber winced. "Do you really have to do that?"

"Never leave the enemy at your back. Now, don't stand around. It's not a party," Ronan called out. They hurried after him, stopping outside an elaborate door that wasn't quite closed.

Amber could feel Paili on the other side. "She's in there." Her words were a whisper.

Ronan pushed the door open. Paili held a large egg. Two Gold Warriors stepped out of the Void behind her. After a glance towards Paili, they started forward.

"I wouldn't if I was you. Unless you want scrambled egg." Ronan stepped forward. "Jasper! Amber!"

Amber raised her hands, fire pooling in them. She searched the egg with her mind and her mouth dropped open with what she found. "It's a Gold Dragon. A little girl. You can't kill a baby." The fire disappeared from her hands. Jasper lowered his hands too.

Everything went crazy. The two warriors attacked Rian and Crystal. Ronan and Kade leapt in, becoming dragons. Amber and Jasper were unable to throw fireballs without hurting someone. Flinn flew in the open door and joined in, trying to protect Crystal. With all the confusion, Paili headed for a small door on the other side of the room.

Anger rushed through Amber. She wasn't about to

let Paili escape. "Jasper. Follow." She turned into a goshawk and flew across the room, landing in front of Paili as a human. Jasper landed behind Paili.

"My children will avenge this. You can't attack whoever you want, regardless of how you feel about me." Paili continued to cradle the egg.

"You started this," Amber said. "My weight in gold."

Paili showed a moment of surprise before her usual haughty expression returned. "You have no proof. Without proof, this will be an unprovoked attack."

Amber grinned. "Now that's where you're wrong."

"I don't believe you. None of my people would betray me."

"Jasper, save the baby." Amber glanced towards him and he nodded. She moved at the same time as Jasper. She threw herself at Paili, becoming a goshawk and going for the eyes. Paili automatically tried to protect herself. Jasper wrenched the egg from her, landing on his side as he protected it from impacting with the floor.

Unencumbered, Paili grabbed hold of Amber who became human to try and fight her. It was impossible. The woman was stronger and pressed her into the ground, a hand at her throat as she tried to cut off Amber's air supply. The sound of fighting still filled the room and Amber knew there was only her and her brother. Everyone else was busy.

She pushed her hands between herself and Paili, starting to feel light headed. *"At the heart,"* she ordered Jasper. Amber filled her hands with fire and forced it into Paili. Her vision went hazy then a dragon was above her, roaring in pain. Amber rolled out of the way as the dragon came down where she'd lain. Scrambling to her feet, she lifted her hands, filling them with fire. Jasper was off to the side, his hands in front of him.

"No, Jasper. Kade and Rian are over there," Amber shouted.

"Amber!" Ronan, in human form, slid a sword across the floor towards her.

She dived out of the way of Paili's wild attack, grabbing the weapon as she rolled past it. Struggling to her feet, she spun to face Paili as the dragon came at her again. Amber hefted the sword, wondering what to do with it. She didn't even have a clue how to use it. An image burst in her mind from Ronan and she shifted her stance, sending fire down the blade as she drove it upwards, straight into Paili's heart.

Fire burst around Amber as Paili roared. Blood flowed down the sword to coat Amber's hands and arms. The fire singed the hair on her arms and heated her stomach and legs that were protected by dragon-leather. Paili collapsed forward, dragging her to the ground. Ronan reached her side, pushing against Paili so Amber could clamber to her feet. He pulled the sword from Paili, holding it out to her.

Confused, Amber took the weapon, resting the tip on the ground so she could lean against it. Exhaustion tugged on her and she fingered the topaz that hung at her throat, drawing power from it. Across the room, Crystal leaned against Flinn while Rian and Kade stood over Paili's two warriors who knelt on the ground in human form. A glance in the other direction showed Jasper cradled the egg.

Ronan grinned at Amber. "To the victor go the spoils." His words filled the room.

The two warriors, heads bent, rose and came to kneel in front of Amber. "Mistress, the castle surrenders to you," one of them said.

Amber stared at them, taking a step back. "No. Oh no." She turned to Ronan. "No." She shook her head.

"Well, if you're rejecting their offer of surrender as the one who did the planning, I will accept," Ronan said.

Rian was at her side in seconds. "She never rejected it. Amber has figured out what you tried to do. As

Amber's first warrior I accept the surrender. See to the injured."

"But-"Amber started to say.

"What she's trying to say is we work as a team," Flinn said. "The victory is shared between the Dragon Mages and their Gold Dragons."

"And who here is Jasper's Gold Dragon?" Ronan asked. "Shannon wasn't in this fight."

Amber wanted to tell everyone to shut up for a minute. She needed time to think, but Paili's two warriors were still there and Ronan was plotting as usual. How could she deal with a castle? She could barely handle the thought of a five bedroom house. Kade, Flinn, Jasper and Crystal moved to stand beside her.

Kade slid an arm around Amber's waist. "If the heir is in residence you have ten minutes to remove him. Close the door behind you."

The two warriors hurried out of the room, shutting the door. Amber pulled away from Kade, turning to Ronan now there was no one else to witness. She hoped. Keeping her gaze on Ronan, she asked, "Is the room clear, Crystal?"

"Yeah. No one playing hide and seek."

"What are you trying to do, Ronan? This isn't your castle."

"It belongs to a seven-year-old. Paili believes only Gold can inherit. She has several children, but she disinherited them all in favour of her only child born Gold. If you leave it in his hands, the first dragon who comes along will own it. How well do you think he could defend the place? As it is, before morning every other castle she owned will be in the hands of someone else. Probably those of her clan. This one we can claim. No one would support the kid."

Amber glared at Ronan. "So we just kick him out of his home? And what about her daughter?"

"They can take the unhatched egg with the boy. But no one will bother with her. She wouldn't be worth their time."

"She's a baby!"

"Forget about the egg. Who gets the castle?" Flinn pointed towards Ronan. "He'll have a castle at the end of the year. He doesn't need this one too."

"What does it matter who gets it?" Ronan asked. "It's another test done for you anyway."

"Test? But don't you have to get approval first?" Amber looked from Flinn to Ronan.

Ronan nodded. "That was Flinn's condition for using Crystal."

"We were waiting around for approval?" Amber demanded.

"No. We had approval. We were waiting for Paili to come here. I knew she wouldn't go into hiding without the egg," Ronan said. "And I had to make sure she thought she needed to hide. I wanted her to believe that I knew what she'd done and was coming for her. But I wanted her to think it was only me coming after her. I didn't want her too well prepared."

"Who gets the castle," Flinn asked again.

Amber turned on him. "Forget the castle!"

Rian rested a hand on Amber's shoulder and she immediately shrugged him off. "What was the test?"

"To avenge an insult," Ronan said.

"To what?" Amber couldn't believe she'd heard correctly. "An insult?"

Ronan nodded.

"An insult?" Her voice was louder.

"We were only kidnapped. That is considered an insult."

Anger swirled through Amber and her hand tightened on the grip of the sword. "An insult." Each word was clearly spoken.

Ronan smiled. His predator smile. "Do you still reject the castle?"

Amber tried to fight the anger that filled her. She had to think clearly. It was impossible. The blood coating her hands and arms reminded her of the nightmares she'd suffered. An insult! What she wanted was to tear Paili apart with her hands. To tan her hide and wear it so everyone could see what would happen to anyone who tried that again. She felt the panther almost pace in her. When someone started to take the sword from her she turned angrily on them, only to let it go when she saw it was Rian. She turned to Ronan. What was the question again? "Was that your plan?"

"It was always a consideration." Ronan shrugged. "You need to learn not to blurt out the first thought that comes into your head."

"How kind of you. Were you worried I wouldn't learn enough today since I cut school to be here?" She eyed Ronan. "You don't look anything like my usual teachers."

"What about the castle? That is the issue here, not any other crap," Flinn said.

"Shut. Up." Amber glared at Flinn.

Flinn ignored her. "Kade, do something with your mage. She's starting to annoy me."

"You're the one annoying everyone, Flinn." Amber held her hand out. "Give me my sword back, Rian."

Ronan started to laugh. "How about we share it?"

"You're to have nothing to do with this land or we don't need to gain you the other lands you want," Flinn said.

"I didn't have to help you with Paili," Ronan said.

"Yes, you did." Kade crossed his arms over his chest. "And you know it."

"Why did he?" Amber asked.

"Because Paili didn't want Ronan to gain any power. To prevent it, she targeted you, Amber," Kade said.

"This was all because of you?" Amber turned to Ronan. When he didn't answer, she stepped close to him. "Your fault?"

"If you want to get right down to it, we could blame my son Tory. Or do you prefer to make me the bad guy?"

Chapter Twenty-Four

Amber didn't know what to think. She was tired, hungry and the blood was drying on her arms and making her even more uncomfortable. "No," she said softly. She turned away and started to pace. "But what are we going to do with a castle?"

Crystal grinned. "Live in it?"

Amber paused in front of her friend. "Seriously?"

Crystal excitedly grabbed Amber's hands then made a face, dropping them the moment she touched the blood. "Yuck! You need a bath."

"Can't anyone around here focus for more than a second at a time?" Flinn threw his hands up. "I'm surrounded by goldfish."

"Do you think it has a ballroom where I can have my seventeenth birthday? I really want a castle," Crystal said. "Pleeeease."

Amber grinned, her anger starting to fade in the

face of Crystal's excitement. "I thought I'd already given you a lifetime of presents." She heard Flinn start to talk again and then the sounds of scuffling behind her, but decided to ignore them. She didn't want to know what was going on as long as someone kept Flinn quiet.

"Well, I need somewhere to keep my pretty rock. Flinn complains if I carry it around."

Amber laughed. "And you think a castle will be big enough to keep it in?"

"This is my dream." Crystal waved to the walls around her. "Ever since we stayed at Kade's family's castle I've wanted one. Can't you picture me as a princess?"

"We don't have princesses or-" Flinn's words were cut off with a grunt and more scuffling.

Crystal giggled as her gaze was drawn to the scene behind Amber. "Say yes before Flinn ends up more battered by his allies than he was by his enemies."

"I guess-" Amber started to say.

Crystal squealed, throwing her arms around Amber. "Eww." She drew back. "I forgot about the blood."

"Finally," Flinn muttered from behind Amber.

"But how can we live here and in our world at the same time?" Amber asked.

"We don't. We finish off the year in your world and our first warriors run things while we're away," Kade said.

"But I don't have any warriors," Crystal said.

"It doesn't matter. Flinn and I will have our warriors take care of things," Kade said.

"No! You're not leaving Maira in charge of things," Flinn ordered.

"Can we forget the castle for a minute and discuss this egg?" Jasper asked.

"No," Flinn said at the same time as Ronan said, "Just scramble it."

Both Amber and Crystal cried, "No!"

"Well, you can't let her be born here. I'll take her if you want," Ronan said.

"I don't trust you with her," Crystal said.

"How do you look after an egg?" Amber asked.

"Can anyone do it?" Jasper moved forward to join the group now the arguing had stopped.

"They just have to be kept at the right temperature," Rian said. "Are you thinking of becoming a father?"

Amber grinned at the expression on Jasper's face. She decided to rescue her brother. "What about Isleen?"

Rian grinned momentarily. "Maybe I should have

chosen something larger if you are planning on turning your house into an orphanage."

"Can we finish sorting out the castle now?" Flinn's words were filled with exaggerated patience.

"Can't we do that later? I really need a shower and something to eat," Amber said.

Ronan shook his head. "We have to be united once we step out that door. The slightest hint of weakness and we might as well slit our own throats."

"What do you want, Ronan?"

"How nice of you to ask, Amber."

"Now who's making everything a drama?"

Ronan smiled as she reworded what he'd previously said to her. "I'm guessing if I say a share in the castle someone is going to complain."

"I will," Flinn said.

"We can still claim it as our lands for the test at the end of a year. Even with this amount of Golds owning it," Kade said.

"Don't I share my mage with him? Why should I have to share my lands with him too?" Flinn demanded.

"What does holding the lands involve?" Jasper asked.

"Killing anyone who tries to take them," Ronan said.

Rian shook his head. "Preventing others from getting them from you. And if Flinn and Kade hold the lands for a full year, they pass the highest Gold Warrior test. It will mean they can become head of their own clans once they have passed a total of ten tests."

"You're starting to confuse me." Amber looked from Rian to Ronan. "You're not Gold and yet you can hold land."

"I can hold as much land as I want, but I can't have my own clan or even be one of the two hundred Representatives or part of the Assembly or Council. And I can never be one of the twenty-five Elders. Not without Gold or at least a child of my own with Gold."

"Can't you adopt?" Amber asked.

Ronan shook his head. "They have to be of my blood too."

"Well, that sucks for you," Amber said.

"Apparently," Ronan said dryly.

"Can we focus for five bloody minutes?" Flinn demanded.

"Why do you need this castle?" Amber asked Ronan.

"So I can recall all the warriors Paili has supporting other people," Ronan said.

"We can recall them and allow you to talk with them about what defences are on your lands," Rian said.

"I never said there were any on my lands. I just want to reduce the support she has in different places," Ronan said.

"Playing games isn't going to get this dealt with quickly and if we take too long I'm going to start thinking you're dinner," Amber warned Ronan.

"She has a mean bite," Rian said.

Amber ignored his comment. "What exactly do you want? No games. Forget about all your stupid negotiating. If it's reasonable I won't argue it."

"Why should we give him everything he wants?" Flinn demanded.

Amber and Ronan turned on Flinn at the same time. "Shut. Up."

Flinn turned to Kade. "Do you really expect me to listen to someone who's exactly like Ronan?"

"I'm not warning you again," Ronan growled.

"You promised not to harm any of us," Flinn said.

Ronan slowly smiled as he stalked close to Flinn, standing in his personal space. "It'll only harm you if you struggle. If you've been warned and you still chose to struggle I'll believe you want that harm."

Flinn met Ronan's gaze, but he remained quiet.

Ronan let the silence stretch out for a full minute. "All troops recalled to this castle. If we move quickly we can claim some of them that have been stationed at this castle previously, but actually belong to other castles owned by Paili. I reserve the right to interrogate any warrior here, be able to reside here when I wish until my own lands are returned to me and use the resources of this castle to help gain that result."

Amber looked towards Rian, unsure what she should say. *"Think you can help out here?"*

Rian smiled fleetingly. "Interrogation will not cause pain or harm to the warriors. You will be respectful to the owners of the castle when residing here and access to the resources to help regain your own lands will not negatively impact upon this castle."

"Those amendments are bearable," Ronan said, still in Flinn's space. "What do you say, Flinn?"

"Whose names will the castle be in?"

"Mine. Oh, it better be mine too." Crystal was just about bouncing on the spot.

"How about everyone in this room except myself and the egg?" Ronan asked.

"Rian isn't Gold," Flinn said.

"You don't have to be Gold to hold a castle," Ronan said.

"He's your son."

"He's Amber's warrior."

"He was your son first."

"Are you saying he didn't help capture this castle? That he didn't put in as much effort as you, Flinn?" Ronan demanded.

"He's just a warrior."

"No, he's not." Amber strode forward to stand beside Ronan, sick of the class distinctions in the dragon lands. "I want him to have a share too."

Flinn turned to Amber. "He's trying to trick you. Rian will no longer be your warrior. He'll have land. Who'll serve you then?"

"Amber-" Rian began.

She waved Rian quiet and met Ronan's gaze. "He'll still be one of mine. You won't be able to harm him."

Ronan grinned. "Is that all that's worrying you? What about less land to own? Who'll guard your back while Rian is seeing to his affairs here?"

Amber matched his grin. "I've got a business card at home of a Gold who'll be looking for a job in less than three months."

Ronan laughed. "Done. He's yours. Paid in full for the rest of his current service."

Amber's grin evaporated. "But I didn't want another warrior," she wailed.

Ronan slung an arm around her shoulders as he turned her to face the rest of the group, lowering his voice. "I know." He raised his voice. "Is everyone in agreement now?" When everyone nodded, said yes or, in Crystal's case, squealed excitedly, Ronan said, "Then let's find some food for Amber. I'm too old to make a decent main meal."

Amber tried to follow everyone from the room, but Ronan held her back. Kade paused in the doorway, waiting for her. She waved him on when Ronan said, *"Chase him away, or should I?"*

When they were alone, with the door closed, Amber pulled away from Ronan. "What now? Don't tell me you've found another assassin who is trying to track me down?"

Ronan shook his head. "Within days everyone will know Paili was behind that offer and you personally killed her." He strode towards the dead dragon.

"Then what do you want to tell me?"

Ronan's predatory smile slowly formed and he drew a dagger from his boot to kneel in front of Paili. He removed the heart and laid it on the floor. It was cut nearly in two. "I once said I'd bring you the heart of the next dragon I slayed. But this is even better. It is the heart of the one you killed." He started cutting the heart into even pieces.

"What are you doing?"

Ronan held up a piece of Paili's heart. Blood stained his hands as he rose to his feet. "What does it look like I'm doing, Amber?"

She tried to ignore the wave of nausea that returned. "Are you sure you don't want a fork and a dinner plate as well?"

"One-twentieth. It's all you need." He continued to hold the piece of heart out to her.

Amber shook her head, looking away as Ronan ate it instead. "One-" she turned back to face him. "You tricked us!"

"Not at all. I said one entire heart and you were all happy to agree. I've just had one twentieth of that heart."

"But that wasn't what we meant."

"Then you should have said what you meant." He grinned slyly. "Surely you didn't expect me to read your minds."

"Damn it, Ronan. This is going to piss off a lot of people. They didn't expect you to live forever."

"Then don't tell them. Let them find out on their own."

"Are you telling me I can't tell them?"

"I'm suggesting you don't. No one likes the bearer of bad news. I've even been known to kill the messenger before and I know I'm not the only one. But it's completely up to you. As I said, they'll find out eventually."

"How?"

Ronan gestured towards the heart. "Unless they can't count."

Amber's eyes narrowed. "And everyone thinks I go looking for trouble. What are you planning, Ronan?"

"Sometimes I like to roll the dice and see how they fall. Just to keep things interesting."

"Well they're far too interesting without random dice rolls." Amber spun, throwing fireballs at the heart. She increased the heat until she had it hot enough to turn the heart to ashes. The room was filled with the stench of burnt flesh when she turned back to Ronan. "Sorry to ruin your fun."

Ronan shrugged. "I'm sure there'll be more."

Amber stared at him certain he spoke the truth. "Where did you get the sword from?"

"I brought it with me."

"Did you plan for me to kill her? How did you know it'd be me?"

"Sometimes a gamble pays off."

"Are you annoyed you didn't get a share of the castle?"

"Are you so certain I didn't?"

Amber thought over his words for a moment. "Is Rian still yours?" She almost dreaded the answer.

"No. He's definitely your man. But he's still my son. And that's what will stay in most people's minds."

Amber smiled. "And you'll make use of their belief."

Ronan nodded. "Of course. Why waste an advantage?"

"If you feel that way, why not let people know you have some Gold in you?"

"Because I can't currently prove there's Gold in my lineage."

"I saw it."

"I wasn't born Gold."

Amber frowned. "Then why are you starting to go Gold? Is it age?"

"No. Experimentation. And until I'm completely Gold I won't let anyone know." Ronan smiled slowly, excitement lighting his eyes. "Can you imagine the amount of people who'll want to see me dead then?"

Amber started to speak but was interrupted by her brother. *"Mum will ring in a second. I've just convinced her I left my phone behind in the library and someone thought it was funny to ring my last called number and tell them I was in hospital. When you asked if Mum had been informed they said she was on the way and said not to bother you about it. You're at the hospital, I just got my phone back and rang you. Maira, who you convinced to give you a lift, will bring you home."*

Amber pulled her phone out of her jacket pocket when it started to ring. *"Thanks. She's ringing now."* She didn't know where her phone went when she changed form and she really didn't want to know. "Hi, Mum."

"How could you be so stupid?"

"Don't start. What was I to expect? It was Jay's phone. Of course I thought it was real. I've spent the last four hours worried about him and thinking you were being an even bigger bitch than usual."

"I want you to come straight home."

Amber sighed heavily, making sure her mother could hear her. "We'll have something to eat first. And a break. You can't expect Maira to drive nearly eight hours with no rests."

"Very well. Give me a call when you're leaving."

"Okay. Bye, Mum."

"Next time, ring me first before you go racing off. Or ring the hospital and make sure it's a real call. I'll see you tonight."

Amber tucked her phone away when her mother disconnected. She faced Ronan. "You cause me all kinds of problems."

Ronan grinned. "It looks like you have it under control."

"Only because Jay comes up with brilliant solutions."

"That boy has the mind of a dragon. Are you sure there aren't any dragons amongst your ancestors?"

"I really hope not." Amber couldn't help thinking about the armoury she'd found at her grandmother's. She firmly put that thought aside. There were far too many other problems to sort without worrying about what that meant. Her stomach grumbled. "Didn't you say something about food earlier?"

Ronan draped an arm around her. "I offered you something to eat and you turned it down."

Amber shuddered as they walked towards the door. "I want real food."

"Your wish is my command."

"Huh! Not very likely."

Chapter Twenty-Five

Amber shut her bedroom door, leaning against it. She closed her eyes, trying to relax after the lecture she'd endured from her mother. She was exhausted. It was over ten hours since Ronan had interrupted her lunch with his demands, but it felt like a year had passed instead.

"Can I get you anything?"

Amber opened her eyes to stare at Alsandair. "I'm fine."

Rian entered the French doors. "She is not fine, but she will become annoyed if you do not believe her."

"Why are you here?" Amber pointed at Rian.

"Because he needs to be taught how to be your warrior." Rian gestured towards Alsandair.

Amber shook her head, not wanting to know any more. It all seemed like too much drama. She glanced around her room. "Where's Kade?"

"As soon as he finishes giving Maira her orders he will come here."

Amber nodded then headed for the bathroom. She saw clothes had been put on the vanity for her to wear to bed. While she was in there, she used the last bit of her power to fill some of her depleted jewellery. She shouldn't need it at least until the morning. She hoped. A night of peace would be good. Peace! Who was she kidding? It didn't look like that was ever likely to be a part of her life.

If the dragon world wouldn't quit hassling her then she was going to make sure they couldn't walk all over her. Amber grabbed her toothbrush, staring at herself in the mirror. She had killed a person. Well, Paili had been a dragon at the time. A close examination showed no changes. Other than the fact she looked completely exhausted.

Amber did her teeth, turning out the light as she entered her bedroom. She paused in the doorway when she saw Kade sprawled on her queen-sized bed. He moved over slightly and she smiled. Not that it'd help much when he fell asleep and transformed into a dragon. She wondered if her grandmother would complain if she replaced the bed with a king-sized one. She couldn't help smiling. Her grandmother would probably buy the bed herself if she thought Amber could use it to get Kade to the altar.

"Should I ask what thoughts are making you smile like that?" Kade asked.

Amber shook her head as she crossed the room, dropping onto the bed. "Absolutely not."

"How are you? Are you sure you shouldn't have asked Ronan to be here tonight?"

"We can't leave the castle completely undefended. He's needed there for now."

"Yes, but-"

Amber pressed her fingers against his lips. "I was wondering, how do they test us on today? I mean, for the wyvern nest they were all over the place."

"They're not stupid enough to get that close, but they will interview the defeated. There should be no problem with passing the test. There were only a handful of us at the end. We can almost claim the rest as diversions."

"Did you know Flinn asked for them to test us on today?"

Kade shook his head. "No, but I should have realised. He'll grab any chance to pass another test."

"Capture a Pliethin, clean out a wyvern nest and avenge an insult." She couldn't stop the anger that filled her as she mentioned the last test. "That's three done. Seven more to go. What's the quickest anyone has ever done all the tests?"

"Nineteen months." Kade grinned. "Try and keep that competitive streak of yours under control. It's pretty tough getting them all done that quick."

"But then Flinn wouldn't be considered clanless. I worry about Crystal."

"Crystal will be fine. You won't allow anything else."

Amber grinned. "Nope." Her grin turned into a yawn that she tried to suppress.

"Time to sleep." Kade tugged her close.

"I guess." She was reluctant to sleep.

"Shh. I'll be right here if you need me."

Amber smiled, pulling him closer so she could kiss him. Anger and thoughts of battle receded. Reluctantly she pulled away. "Goodnight."

Kade smiled slightly. "Sweet dreams."

Rian turned the light out and Amber rested her head against Kade's shoulder. She worried what her dreams would bring after the battle she'd seen that day. Sweet was probably going to be the last word to describe them. She tried to think of something else to distract herself with and the locked doors down the hallway came to mind.

It was tempting to find out more about them. But

did she really want to? Could she handle any more secrets in her life? Probably not. It was safer to leave them locked. Safer to try and control her curiosity a little better. Maybe that just might keep her out of trouble more often. Yeah, right. Who was she kidding? She finally drifted off to sleep, unable to stay awake any longer. Her dreams were filled with waves crashing against a rocky shoreline and a parade of people who called out, "Long live the Queen." She would have almost preferred oceans of blood.

Free Ebook

Subscribe to Avril's newsletter and receive a free ebook. This ebook is exclusive to those on her mailing list. To find out more about this offer visit:

www.avrilsabine.com/free-ebook

*

We value your privacy and will not sell, rent, exchange or loan your email address to third parties. Your information is confidential and you are under no obligation to remain on the mailing list and can unsubscribe at any time.

Acknowledgements

Thank you to my usual crew for putting in excessive hours to help me improve this series.

To The Reader

If you enjoyed this book, why not consider leaving a review to help other readers discover it too? Reader engagement is one of the few ways that lets an author know readers want more books in a particular series or genre. So leave a review and tell friends, not only about this book but also about other ones you've enjoyed, so you can continue to enjoy books by your favourite authors for years to come.

Dreams are meant to be lived,

Avril.

About The Author

Avril is an Australian author who lives with her family on acreage in South East Queensland. She writes mostly young adult and children's speculative fiction, but has been known to dabble in other genres. You can find more information about her at www.avrilsabine.com where you can also subscribe to her newsletter to be kept informed about new releases, current projects, blog posts and exclusive news.

Titles By Avril Sabine

Stories about strong characters and characters who discover their strengths.

SERIES

Assassins Of The Dead- Young Adult Fantasy/ Paranormal

Book 1: Dark Blade

Book 2: Dragon Touched

Book 3: Society Against Vampires

Book 4: King's Request

Dragon Blood- Young Adult Urban Fantasy (with elements of romance)

(5 book series)

Book 1: Pliethin

Book 2: Wyvern

Book 3: Surety

Book 4: Knight

Book 5: Mage

Dragon Mage- Young Adult Urban Fantasy (with elements of romance)

(Series two of Dragon Blood series)

Book 1: Promise

Dragon Blood Chronicles- Young Adult Urban Fantasy (with elements of romance)

(Companion stand alone series to Dragon Blood)

Book 1: Oath

Book 2: Betrayed

Guardians Of The Round Table- Young Adult Fantasy LitRPG

(Co-written with Storm and Rhys Petersen)

Book 1: Dexterity Fail

Book 2: Goblin Boots

Book 3: Singed Feathers

Book 4: Frog Mage

Book 5: Crystal Mine

Book 6: Cursed Harp

Rosie's Rangers- Young Adult Western Steampunk

(6 book series)

Book 1: Justice

Book 2: Vengeance

Book 3: Treachery

Book 4: Accused

Book 5: Wanted

Book 6: Corruption

Mark Of Kings- Children's Fantasy

(Upper middle grade/preteen)

(4 book series)

Book 1: The Arena

Book 2: The Island

Book 3: The Assassin

Book 4: The King

STAND ALONE SERIES

Demon Hunters- Young Adult Urban Fantasy/ Horror (with elements of romance)

Book 1: Blood Sacrifice

Book 2: Retribution

Book 3: Tainted

Book 4: Premonition

Book 5: Cursed

Book 6: Feud

Book 7: Extrication

Plea Of The Damned- Young Adult Urban Fantasy/Paranormal

(6 book series)

Book 1: Forgive Me Lucy

Book 2: Forgive Me Aiden

Book 3: Forgive Me Jena

Book 4: Forgive Me Kobe

Book 5: Forgive Me Marti

Book 6: Forgive Me Dawson

Realms Of The Fae- Young Adult Urban Fantasy (with elements of romance)

The Sword (short story in Like A Girl Anthology)

Heart Of Stone

Book 1: A Debt Owed

Book 2: Marked By The Hunt

Book 3: The Magic Collector

Book 4: An Unexpected Betrayal

Book 5: Imprisoned By Iron

Fairytales Retold (Short Stories)

Snow-White And Rose-Red

The Twelve Brothers

The Light Princess

Beauty And The Beast

Sleeping Beauty

Aschenputtel

The Golden Bird

The Frog Prince

The Death Of Koshchei The Deathless

Myths And Legends Retold (Short Stories)

Ion, Son Of Apollo

Sir Gawain And The Maid With The Narrow Sleeves

Princess Ilse, The Giant's Daughter

YOUNG ADULT NOVELS

Young Adult Fantasy (with elements of romance)

Elf Sight

Earth Bound

Young Adult Urban Fantasy

Stone Warrior (with elements of romance)

The Jungle Inside

Young Adult Contemporary (with elements of romance)

Through Your Eyes

The Ugly Stepsister

Perfect Little Princess

Young Adult Contemporary/Paranormal

Whispers In The Dark (with elements of romance and same sex relationships)

Over Too Soon (with elements of romance)

Young Adult Sci-Fi

Experiment X-One-Six (Urban Sci-Fi/Superheroes)

An Endless Dawn (Post Apocalyptic Sci-Fi)

CHILDREN'S BOOKS

Dragon Lord (Preteen/early teens) (Fantasy)

The Irish Wizard (Upper middle grade) (Urban Fantasy)

SHORT STORIES

Urban Fantasy

Eternally Late

Dealings With Joe

Glimpses (short story in That Moment When
Anthology)

Contemporary

The Brat Next Door

Fantasy LitRPG

(Set in the same world as Guardians Of The Round
Table Series)

Tales Of Inadon 1: The Disc (Co-written with
Storm and Rhys Petersen) (short story in Game On!
Anthology)

Post Apocalyptic Sci-Fi

Compulsive Directive

NONFICTION

A Year Of Weekly Writing Exercises (Creative Writing)

Cooking For Families With Allergies (Cooking) (Co-written with Storm Petersen)

Tell Me A Story, Grandma (Memoir)

For the most up to date details on available titles visit:

www.avrilsabine.com/books/bibliography

Dragon Blood Series

To learn more about this series visit:

www.avrilsabine.com/series/db

BOOKS AVAILABLE IN THE DRAGON BLOOD SERIES

(5 book series)

Book 1: Pliethin

Book 2: Wyvern

Book 3: Surety

Book 4: Knight

Book 5: Mage

BOOKS SET IN THE SAME WORLD AS THE DRAGON BLOOD SERIES

Dragon Mage- Young Adult Urban Fantasy (with elements of romance)

(Series two of Dragon Blood series)

Book 1: Promise

Dragon Blood Chronicles- Young Adult Urban Fantasy (with elements of romance)

(Companion stand alone series to Dragon Blood)

Book 1: Oath

Book 2: Betrayed

Disclaimer

This is a work of fiction. Names, characters, businesses, places, events and incidents are either the products of the author's imagination or used in a fictitious manner. Any resemblance to actual persons, living or dead, or actual events is purely coincidental. The opinions expressed or beliefs held are those of the characters and should not be assumed to be the opinions or beliefs of the author.